WAXWING CREEK

WAXWING CREEK

J.J. WALKER

WAXWING CREEK

Cover art: Matt Seff Barnes Art

Editor: Renee DeCamillis

Interior design: J.J. Walker

jjwalkerwrites.com

Paperback ISBN: 978-1-7389906-2-7

Ebook ISBN: 978-1-7389906-3-4

This isn't a story about a motel.

This isn't a story about ghosts.

This is a story about people, which may be the scariest thing of all.

AUTHOR'S NOTE

Waxwing Creek is not a pleasant place. Its history is filled with murder, suicide, abuse, and other maladies that make us human. While its legacy spans decades, and its walls are stained with conversations and deeds both unspeakable and unforgivable, the ones you are about to discover are its most defining. Perhaps its most disturbing.

You have been warned.

AN ULTIMATUM

1989

IT WASN'T until Brett Roberts asked Cliff to spell his name for a second time that he mustered the strength to pull the letters together. The night had been long and he was tired. Grieving.

"C-L-I-F-F-H-O-W-A-R-D," he said, head throbbing.

"Alright, Cliff. And you're the owner of Waxwing Creek?"

"That's right."

"You don't just own the motel. You live there?"

"Correct."

The detective sighed, tapping chubby fingers with nails still stained with breakfast's syrup on the table's surface.

"Alright. You live there with your wife? With Annabelle?"

"We didn't do it." The words came fast. His eyes looked anxious and angry. "Me or Anna. We just found her like that." Cliff started to panic. "I don't know what happened."

"Cliff."

"I swear it." Cliff's face broke apart. His cheeks filled with a red so bright it throbbed on his face. He forced himself to loosen his hands, which were gripped around the table's edge.

"Cliff!" The detective's voice echoed around the small room, cutting everything off except the sound of tape spinning. "We just want to get to the facts. We've already spoken with your wife. She did fine. Now you get to tell your side of the story. Think you can do that for me?"

Cliff nodded, rubbing his eyes with the heels of his hands.

"Which one of you decided to build the motel?"

"It was mutual. We both wanted it, for different reasons. Anna used to work in a diner. She loved that job. Said there was nothing better than bringing people pancakes and seeing their faces light up in the morning. She had an eye for that sort of stuff. Hospitality. Whether it's the pens at the front desk or the carpets in the rooms, every detail in that motel is there because *she* decided it. She's in the business of making life a little easier for folks. Even the name, Waxwing Creek. She chose that. Always loved the way those birds look. How social they are. Likes that name so much she put a note in the deed begging future owners not to change it."

"And you?"

Cliff thought about the motel. Thought about its rooms lined up, waiting. The dusted earth that passed as a parking lot. He thought about the forest that surrounded it, wounded, as though they'd carved out a place for it in the trees. He thought of the chairs they'd placed outside every room, where guests could sit and look out at the long road stretching out of Hunt. He thought about the metal sign that invaded that road, its tall letters reading: WAXWING CREEK MOTEL.

"I just wanted to make her happy."

The detective grunted.

"How many rooms?"

"Seven."

"Ground floor?"

"Ground floor," Cliff said.

"Were you aware of its history? Did you know what happened on that land before you built it?"

"Sure," Cliff said, eyes down. "We heard the stories."

"What stories did you hear, Cliff?"

"You're from Hunt."

"So?"

"So, you'll know the stories as well as anyone, Detective."

Brett sighed. "But I'm here to find out what *you* know, Cliff. Your take on those stories is an important part of what happened tonight, wouldn't you agree? I'd like to revisit them for the record. Hear them from you."

Cliff let out a groan. "Dakota House. The motel was built on top of what was once Dakota House. Before we tore it down."

"And what happened at Dakota House?"

"Come on, man. This isn't relevant."

"Cliff. What happened?"

"A whole family died there. Mother, father, three kids. Shot in the attic. Most put it down to murder. Some said it was ghosts. It's a mystery nobody got to the bottom of, is what I'm trying to say."

"How did that feel? Building a motel on top of a tragedy like that?"

"I mean, we talked about it. Thought about it...a lot," he said. "But the way we saw it, that was years ago. Place had been empty since. And honestly? We would have never been able to afford it if it was anywhere else."

Cliff watched the detective push back into his seat, resting those chubby fingers on top of his protruding belly. The man had told Cliff his name, some other things about his rights and what they intended to do. He couldn't remember any of it. The last thing he remembered was the light of the officer's car soaking the walls with blue as blood had soaked their carpet red, and then his head had been pushed into the back of the cruiser.

"Did you want more water?"

Cliff looked down at the paper cup, unaware he'd emptied it. "I'm good," he said.

"Alright. So, you and Annabelle built the motel. Did you live in it from the beginning?"

"No. We lived in a small apartment nearby. On Elk Avenue."

"What made you move?"

"Money," Cliff said, matter of fact. "Not enough of it."

"Was that a hard decision?"

"Yes."

"Mutual?"

"Eventually. I had to talk Anna into it. Sure, we'd save on rent, but it also meant cutting into the motel's income, and we'd be living where we worked. We had to make sure what we were doing was right financially."

"So, at what point did you and Annabelle decide things needed to change? When did you decide moving in was the right thing to do?"

THE FORCE of the door slamming lifted the apartment's pictures from the walls.

"Anna? What's the matter?"

"I don't know how we're going to do it."

"Do what?"

"Survive!" Annabelle stepped over the empty wine bottles and newspapers, throwing her bag to the floor before slumping onto the couch. The apartment was small, with a bedroom that only had enough room for a bed and a few boxes. It hadn't taken long for those boxes to overflow into the living room and kitchen, creating the mess they currently called home.

"Calm down, honey."

"We've not even been open a year, and business is slowing down. The motel has seven rooms, and how many are full right now? One. One! Fresh start my ass."

"Anna, please stop shouting. The neighbors. We'll figure it out."

"And then the shit we have to deal with. The things they do to each other. The things you wish you could *unsee.*"

Cliff sighed. He knew he wasn't going to get through to her. Not tonight. But over the last few weeks, an idea had been brewing. Two ideas, in fact. In that moment, he told himself he'd bring up the first: to move into one of the motel's rooms. The other? He'd only share that if things turned desperate.

"So, you moved into Waxwing Creek."

"Into room one."

"Do you remember the date?"

"January 5th, 1989. We figured it would be a good way to start the new year. A fresh start, you know?"

The detective nodded, checking his watch. "That's nine months ago to the day."

The table in front of Cliff felt more sterile, the walls more suffocating. It was as though their arrival in the motel had impregnated the place with horror, and it had needed all nine months to give birth.

The cassette sounded like it was getting caught on itself. Cliff felt like he might get sick from the continuous sound of grinding plastic.

"Do you need to change the tape?"

"No," Brett said, looking for something around him. "It's just talkative."

Cliff settled, fighting to pull his thoughts from the way the body looked when police arrived. The way its bones had splintered and split the skin, with the white pushed through flesh. The way they'd all been seated around that table minutes before, excited about what could happen next.

He watched the detective working through something out of sight, resting on the chair next to him. When he revealed a copy of *The Hunt Herald* and slid it across the table, open on a specific page, Cliff knew the game was up.

"For the record, I'm presenting Cliff with a clipping from *The Hunt Herald* titled 'The Motel That Dares Mess with Hunt's Haunting Past.' You want to tell me how this idea came about, Cliff?"

***

CLIFF TAPPED his fingers against the mattress. He felt anxious, perched on the bed next to a hand towel he'd just used to wipe the sweat beading his brow. The night was warm. Sticky.

He'd been toying with the idea for weeks. Building it

up. Tearing it apart. Interrogating it limb by limb. If things weren't as desperate as they were, he would have happily and easily pushed the idea so far to the back of his mind it would have rusted and broken down to tiny pieces he could bring to the grave. But things were bad. The situation desperate. Both the motel and his marriage were on the line.

The door erupted from its frame. Annabelle came in carrying a pile of washed clothes.

"Room four," she said. "You do not wanna see the state those boys left it in."

"Anna," Cliff said.

"I just don't get it. How can someone come into someone else's property and leave it like that?"

"Anna."

"Makes me so *angry*."

"Anna!"

"What, Cliff? What do you want?"

"Sit down. I need to talk to you about something."

"I don't have time right now."

Cliff pushed himself off the bed. He rested his hand over one of hers, taking the clothes from her arms with the other. It felt odd, touching her again. It had been so long since they'd embraced, kissed, made love. Clearly it caught her off guard, because he sensed his wife soften and surrender the clothes to him.

He dragged her to the bed, and for a second, he saw the flicker of lust enter her eyes, wondering if she thought he was about to break the unspoken habit they'd established. It would have been easier to do that, but he'd talked himself up to this, so it was only right that he went through with it.

"This isn't working," Cliff said.

"Us or the motel?" Annabelle murmured, moving her eyes away from him.

"The motel," he said, ignoring the sting. "I've been thinking of a way we can...make it right. Try and bring in more business."

"Cliff," Annabelle said with a heavy breath. "If you suggest getting the local papers to stay for free one more time, or leaflets, or a community fucking barbecue, I swear to God..."

"No, no, no," Cliff said. "Nothing like that."

"What then?"

"The Dakotas."

"What about them?"

"Do you ever think about them? Who they were? What they were like?"

"No, Cliff. Why would I do that?"

"Because we chose to build a motel on top of their home. On top of their story. And maybe..." Cliff hesitated. "Maybe it's a story people are interested in."

"What are you suggesting?"

"I don't know. Maybe we could lean into it a bit more. Make it part of our brand. Just for a night."

"I'm not following."

He could tell he was losing her. This was the part where she'd dismiss him. Where she'd stand up, grab the clothes, and leave the room. So he decided to just come out and say it.

"A séance."

"What?"

"I think we should host a séance."

"You think we should host a séance?"

"Yes. Put the word out, say we've been seeing things, hearing things, whatever. Say we can feel the Dakotas here. Then, we invite people to come and experience it themselves. For just one night."

"Are you out of your mind?"

"Honey, think about it. If anything's ever going to put us on the map, get people talking, it's this."

"There's no way."

"Just think about it."

"I've thought about it, and it's a no, Cliff."

"Why not?"

"What you're talking about here is tarnishing *our* legacy. Something we've poured our blood, sweat, and tears into. You're talking about turning the motel into some... tourist attraction. And it isn't even true! I've never seen a ghost, let alone felt a Dakota in here. Have you?" Cliff stared at her, waiting for words that never arrived. "Exactly. I don't know how much you've been drinking, but this is... this is not right."

The pair fell quiet, Cliff with his face to the floor, Annabelle looking at him with tired eyes. The plastic fan Cliff had set up hit the end of its arc, turning back with an artificial creak. The pipes in the motel groaned as a guest in another room turned on the shower.

"Well, we're out of options," he said, defeated. "I'm giving you an ultimatum. Either we try this or I'm gone."

***

THE DETECTIVE HAD BEEN NODDING for the past minute. Cliff knew what he was giving him was good. If Brett solved this, got to the bottom of it, it would bring positive press for the Hunt Police Department and a pat on the back from the boss. Could even lead to a raise.

"So, this séance. It was your idea?" he said.

"It was my idea, but Annabelle came around to it. She was as excited as I was. And it worked, didn't it?" Cliff said, motioning toward the paper on the table. "It got our name out there. Everybody in Hunt was talking about it. Check our books. We have back-to-back reservations for the next *month*."

"Is that right?"

"You think we're the first people to do something like this? I was being smart. Entrepreneurial. Making the most of what we'd been given."

"Alright, alright. So you decided to host a séance. What exactly did you have planned? Did you intend to actually make contact with the Dakotas?"

"That's how we put it out there. How we marketed it. Obviously we never intended for anything that happened tonight to actually happen. I thought you had to believe in spirits to meet spirits. We just planned to put on a bit of a show, create an atmosphere. Let people make their own minds up and, hopefully, walk away with something they'd talk about to bring more people in."

"Cliff," Brett said.

"What?"

"Look at me a second."

He raised his eyes to meet the detective, and saw a face crinkled in confusion. Or was it disgust? "You have got to understand how this sounds. I mean, *come on*, man. Of all the ways to drum up business, you chose a séance?"

Cliff remained silent.

"How many people were there?"

"Seven. Nine including us."

"Were they planning on staying the night?"

"Yes, sir."

"All of them?"

"The first time we'd had a full motel of paying guests in weeks."

"Who were they?"

"You'd have to check the books. I don't remember their names."

"Try, Cliff. A woman has died. Do you have any idea how serious this is?"

"I said I don't remember. There was an old guy, a couple, a young man, a journalist from the paper," he said. "Me and Annie, obviously, and some regular who's been staying at the motel."

"And the victim."

Cliff thought of her. She'd looked anxious but kind. Under her jacket, she'd been wearing a summer dress despite the cold, with hair that stopped below her shoulders. Now she was dead. Her hair and the dress were soaked with blood. He thought of her friends, her family, and felt the guilt of what had happened mounting. At the very least, he should remember her name.

"Of course," Cliff whispered. "And the woman who died."

"Jesus," Brett muttered. "Now, I've never been to a séance, so I'm struggling to..." he stopped, waving fat fingers around his head, "visualize it. Were the lights on or off? Were you sitting or standing? What was the set-up? Help me out here. Tell me as much as you remember, in as much detail as possible."

<hr>

THEY'D DECIDED to do it in Cliff and Annabelle's room. It made sense, given that's where the pair had said they'd come into contact with the Dakotas most. Where they had concocted stories by lamplight: a fist against the spine, a slipped sheet off the bed while they were sleeping. It was all a lie, of course. A means to a better and brighter end.

The bed was pushed against the wall to make room for a large, round, wooden table that filled the room's other side. An unlit candle sat on the tabletop, surrounded by a variety of foods that gave the room a soft aroma. Annabelle had read somewhere that it would help bring spirits into the world of the living if they felt they'd have some nourishment. They'd also managed to find, tucked in the corner of an antique store, a battered Ouija board, its white letters stark on the dark wood, which was set in the table's middle.

Before inviting everybody in, they'd left only the lamps by their bed on, lit the candle, and sat their guests around that table like cogs around a wheel, ready to propel a dying motel back into action. If Cliff ever thought he'd be able to believe in contacting the other side, it was in that moment.

As the guests engaged in nervous chatter, Cliff sat at one side of the table, Annabelle at the other. Both had chosen to wear black to add to the mood, and they'd made a particular effort to dress up for the occasion. Cliff picked a suit he hadn't worn since Annabelle's father's funeral, and Annabelle had selected a long skirt, black and flowing. He sent her a glance, wanting it to comfort her. Judging by the look she gave back, he figured she had received it as something different.

"Good evening, everybody," Cliff began. The chat stilled, and all eyes turned to him. He forced himself to swallow, aware of the nervous heat gathering around his neck. "Myself and my wife, Annabelle, want to thank you all for coming tonight. We deliberated for a long time whether we should attempt what we're about to do here. We know it could be dangerous. We know it could lead to experiences that are new for all of us. So I'm glad we're able to do it together." Cliff paused, taking stock of the room. He wanted to see their reactions, but found they weren't reacting at all. Instead, they were listening. They were looking at him, lapping it up.

He licked his lips.

"From the moment we opened Waxwing Creek, we knew a legacy was at work here. A story to be respected. But we also know that it is a legacy that has remained unsolved for many years. Hopefully," he said, pausing for dramatic effect, "tonight is the night we get some answers."

At that, Cliff had invited everybody to introduce themselves. He discovered a room of believers and skeptics from across the country, all with different reasons for being there, and all, to his surprise, with different stories of how they'd heard about Waxwing Creek.

While Cliff and Annabelle talked about their experiences with the motel, they all shared their own views on what they thought had happened that night at Dakota House. Despite their differences, Cliff noted one thing that united them: they were here to experience something, and they were willing to pay good money to do it.

When the old man next to Cliff had finished his story, saying how he wasn't interested in the Dakotas but rather the opportunity to get a glimpse at death, Cliff stood.

"Thank you, everybody, for sharing that. Now, we will begin." He put his finger on top of the small planchette used to slide across the Ouija board's surface, and encouraged everybody to do the same. Cliff wiped the sweat from his brow and palms and began to speak.

"If the Dakotas are listening, know that we are attempting to make contact in peace. We understand that this is your space. We acknowledge and respect that this motel was built on top of the place you called home. We know that the way your lives ended was sudden, unplanned, tragic, and the land of the living has wronged you in letting your legacy continue without a resolution." Cliff shot a look to Annabelle. When she responded with a smile, he felt encouraged in his performance. He was getting into it, warming up, and told himself not to get carried away.

"So, if there is anyone here, if any of the Dakotas are listening, we would love for you to come forward. We would love for you to tell your side of the story."

The room's silence was so sharp, Cliff wondered if it would prick him. He felt his palms sweating again, and he sensed his finger against the old man's beside him.

"Ask a question," Annabelle said from across the table. "Be specific."

"Okay," Cliff said. "Is there anyone listening? Do we have a spirit in the room with us?"

At first, no one moved. Nothing stirred. Then, the planchette shifted. Around him, the guests gasped, letting out yelps and strained curses when its circle hovered over the *YES*. Cliff hadn't forced it. He hadn't applied any pressure, but was pleased Annabelle had taken the reins.

"Alright," Cliff announced. "Who are we speaking with?"

Again, the planchette moved, gliding its way across the board.

"D," the young woman next to Annabelle whispered. "For Dakota."

"E," her partner said. "Can't be."

As one, the room watched it continue from *E* to *A* to *T*, and then *H*. Each time the planchette's window landed on a letter, someone around the table called it out.

"Death," Cliff whispered, unsettled at where his wife

had decided to take it. He raised his head to meet her eyes, to question what she was doing, but something changed. Cliff felt the force of it enter his finger and realized, from the anxious outbursts around the table, everyone else felt it too. The wood didn't just move, it vibrated.

"Honey?" Cliff hoped Annabelle's eyes would have the answer. When she shouted it wasn't her, he removed his finger along with everybody else and watched as the shaped tile started to move on its own. It picked up pace, like a hockey puck on ice, moving from letter to letter, to *YES*, to *NO*, then it started skirting the board's border. It moved as though it were hurting. Its motions were too quick to follow, its gliding too fast to keep up with. To his left, Cliff felt the old man tense. To his right, someone let out a whimper.

And then the bulbs by the bedside blew out, and the candle extinguished. In one extreme movement, the room was thrown into darkness. Everyone, including Cliff, screamed as the sensation of something unhinged and unholy swept through the room, throwing air that was hot and cold, wet and dry, in every direction.

Around them, the sound of splintering wood filled the air, so loud it was deafening. At first, Cliff thought it was the trees outside in the forest, snapping branches to smother them. Then he wondered whether it was the roof about to buckle under the pressure of the supernatural.

This wasn't a sensation that came and went. It was one that built on itself. With every second that passed, it grew, thrummed, throbbed to the point that Cliff thought it would tear the room in two. As the splintering continued, he couldn't shake the feeling that something out of this world had lifted everything good and pure from his soul. He thought he could hear screaming, but wasn't sure. The splintering was too loud, the cracking too violent.

Then the sound changed, just slightly, and he understood that what he thought was splintering wood was in fact bones, and they turned to wet slaps and guttural screams on the other side of the table. He fought to hear anything other than the thuds of flesh, the endless shouting, thinking he wasn't going to survive. He was convinced, in that moment, that this room would be his end. Room one of Waxwing Creek was where he was going to die.

But then it did fade. The world quieted, and all that was left was a man with his knees tucked under his chin and people sobbing and shivering around him.

"A-A-A-Annie," he said, easing the sounds out as best he could from a dry, tight throat. "Annie, honey. Are you there?"

The sound of her breathing intensified through the gloom's thickness. He tried to push himself out of his chair. As he did, his hand came into contact with the cold skin of the old man beside him.

"Fuck," he whispered. "Annie, I think someone's hurt. Is anybody else awake?"

"I'm awake," someone said.

"Me too," whispered someone else.

"Cliff," Annabelle started to cry. "Oh my God, Cliff."

"Just, everybody, try to stay calm. Don't move. I think the power's out, but there's a flashlight in the office. I'll grab it. Try and reset the fuse box."

"Okay," Annabelle said. "Just be quick. Please."

"I will."

Through sensations of feet and fingers, Cliff found his way to the door, closing his eyes tighter and biting his lip whenever his foot came into contact with something solid. As he reached the outside of the motel, he saw how dark the forest was around them. There were no lights, but still he saw reflections on the leaves, like countless little eyes. He pushed them away, tried to ignore them, continuing his way along the outer wall, forcing himself to take measured breaths until he reached the office. He opened the door and hurried to the desk to grab the flashlight.

He clicked it on, shying from its brightness. He didn't know what awaited him back in their room, but his wife was there. People were hurt. He hurried out of the office, turned the corner, and shone the light into the darkness of room one.

It took a second for Cliff to orient himself. For the flashes of white and red to stitch together an image that made sense. If it wasn't for Annabelle's scream, all of their screams, he didn't know if he'd have ever moved. Later, they'd learn it was those screams, guttural and raw, that prompted someone to call the police. But in that moment, all that mattered was the mess of flesh and bone sitting in place of what was once a woman.

Cliff stumbled past the corpse and tried to haul the sobbing weight of his wife to safety. He tried to make sense of it all. He tried to understand how someone's body could end up so mutilated. Tried to figure out how a body, bruised in purples and blues, had managed to push its bones through its skin.

———

THE DETECTIVE's voice brought Cliff out of the memory, back to the cold room and the cassette that never seemed to end.

"How did you know the victim, Cliff?"

"We didn't know her."

"Are you sure about that? Because my patience is wearing a little thin."

"You're damn right I'm sure."

"So what happened?" Brett said, leaning over the table. "What happened tonight at Waxwing Creek?"

"It was the Dakotas. There's no other explanation. We called on them. Contacted them. And…well, one of them killed her."

"Oh, give me a break."

"I'm telling the truth!"

"And that's your statement, is it? You're going on record to say that you think one of the Dakotas killed that woman?"

"I am."

"And there's nobody else involved?"

"No one."

"Another guest?"

"No."

"Your wife?"

"No!" The volume of Cliff's voice shocked the room into quiet, and the two stared at each other, breathing heavily, taking a moment to compose themselves.

"There is *nothing* else you want to tell us?" Brett began again. "You don't think anyone tonight acted with malicious intent?"

"Detective, you saw that woman's body."

"I did."

"Then you tell me how you think we did it." Cliff spat the words out. "How *any* of us did it. Just how do you think we managed to pull her spine out of her fucking mouth?"

BINGO

1992

Deborah Lark watched the woman at the other side of the room lift her dauber from the paper and shout, "Bingo!"

"Fucking hell," John said, throwing his dauber on the table. "Is she gonna leave some for the rest of us?"

"Oh, stop," Janice said, shaking her head. "You're just mad because you picked the wrong numbers."

"Don't say it like there's skill involved. I don't pick the numbers. You know as well as I do, it's luck. It's *all* luck."

"Well, luck or not, Maggie over there just won. Not you."

"Yeah, yeah. Whatever."

"Deb. How'd you do?"

Deborah looked at her bingo card. Too many numbers stood out on stark white. Not enough in dried stains of blue. Around her, conversation had risen and hands were tearing sheets from pads, ready to go again.

"Not good."

"Well, don't lose faith," Janice said, rolling up her sleeves and taking a deep drink of her beer. "Onto the next."

Deborah closed the door to her room at Waxwing Creek, moving the chain across the lock. Next door, she heard arguing and thumped a flat palm against the wall, yelling at them to shut up. She fumbled in one of the drawers for her lighter, igniting the cigarette gripped between her lips.

Dragging smoke into her lungs, she removed the bills from the back pocket of her jeans before her ass hit the pillow. The bills felt waxy. They made her hands smell unclean. Not enough for a week at Waxwing Creek, but enough for a few more nights of bingo.

As if on cue, the door to her room rattled.

"Yeah, yeah," she said, slipping the money back into her pocket. She unlatched the chain and opened the door to the portly figure of Waxwing Creek's owner, Walt Crane. Behind him sat her old station wagon, unmoved since she'd arrived. Overhead, a flurry of moths hit their bodies against the metal covers protecting the lights. The air felt muggy. Walt's thick mustache spilled over his lips to cover the tops of his teeth, matching the gray sprouts erupting from the sides of his head. She could see his t-shirt had a hole around the collar and a bad stain on the front.

"Walt, I know what you're gonna say. I just..."

"If you know what I'm going to say, then why am I at your door saying it? Come on, Deb. You've been here long enough. I know times are tough. But you're a month over-due, and I'm trying to run a business. I've got bills I gotta pay."

"Walt."

"Don't, Deb. I don't want to hear it. I'm giving you three days, one for every loan my mother gave me to buy this place. And that's only because I'm generous. If your bill ain't settled by midnight on Wednesday, that's it. I don't care if I have to get the cops out here. I don't care if I have to remove you myself. You're *out*."

Deb stared at him. She didn't try to put a look in her eyes or a feeling on her face. She looked at him honestly.

"And put that out, will you?" he said, motioning toward the cigarette. "I don't want my room stinking for whoever's in here next."

She closed the door and slid the lock back in place, pushing against it until she'd finished smoking. She surveyed her room, her home, stretched out in front of her. Clothes piled in corners, heaped over the room's only chair. Her bed was unmade. A television set sat on a table at the end of it, next to the microwave she'd found in a dumpster a month ago. Everything reeked of bad memories and stale smoke.

She'd heard the stories about Waxwing Creek, but that's what made it so cheap. Only desperate people would pay to stay on land where a family was found dead and a séance had gone wrong. She would know. *She* was desperate.

Deborah shuffled into the bathroom. Maybe tonight would be the night she'd end it. The night she would stop running and find the courage to kill herself.

As she faced the mirror, she thought about the day she'd turned her beat up car into the Waxwing Creek lot, engine rattling in its chamber. The motel's metal sign had swung limply in the wind, promising a vacant room. That room, different than the one she was in now, had holes in its walls and spots of blood on the bedsheets. The lights had been artificial, blazing like cold fires.

A week was what she'd promised herself. A week and she'd be out. Only she'd broken that promise. Lied to herself. Pulled the rug from under her own feet. What happened had happened, and as those weeks rolled into months, Waxwing Creek had become her home. Days passed and her desire to move on diminished. The urge to stay on the road vanished.

The bulb above her shone on the mass of curly red hair pulled to the top of her head, highlighting the dark, freckled bags under her eyes. She tried to smile, noting the nicotine stains on her teeth and the white scar on her chin. She thought about who'd given her that scar.

The man she was running from.

"Make your own luck," she said to the mirror, mimicking him, lip pulled up in a snarl. "If you want anything in life, sweetie, make your own luck. Remember that. Make your own *fucking* luck."

And then she saw him. Actually saw him. Saw his face appear in the mirror in front of her, his features dark, his face alert, blooming a rotten smile.

"So do it then," he said, his voice a reminder of everything she'd tried so hard to forget.

Her breath caught. She looked away, turning the tap to full. It sprayed everywhere, soaking her top and running down the walls. She fumbled to turn it off, returning her gaze to the mirror to see the image had disappeared. She was alone again, but she had seen him, heard him, and he looked real.

She'd stayed in a few motels since escaping her husband, but something about Waxwing Creek was different. Here, she saw things. Felt things. At Waxwing Creek, the paranoia had intensified to the point of delusion, and she'd found, with every day that passed, the anxiety of her husband finding her stitched itself deeper. At night, she'd sleep with the light on, scared his face would find its way to her in the darkness. In the day, she'd hear him speaking, muttering, talking about how she should be making her own luck.

Next door, the shouts had turned to sex. Just as loud. Just as violent. As Deborah made her way back to the bed, she didn't thump her fist against the wall. Instead, she lay back and closed her eyes to shut it out. After a while they finished, and sleep arrived. When it did, and she drifted willingly into the darkness, Deborah had her hand clutched around the last bills in her pocket, thinking of the bright lights of bingo.

THEY SANG, those lights. They were fluorescent. Sterile. But still, they sang. Tables spread to the left and right of Deborah like wings, and their chairs were filled with people. To these people, these players, this place was a temple of bright lights. A sanctuary of neon colors in a sad town called Hunt.

"Deb, are you doing okay?" It was Janice. She said it quietly, under her breath, and Deborah felt the warmth of the woman's hand on top of hers.

"Oh, I'm fine," Deborah said, moving her hand away. "I'm just not sleeping well, that's all."

"I hear ya. Where are you coming from?"

"Where am I living?"

"Yeah."

"I'm kind of in between places. Trying to figure a few things out."

"Say no more," Janice said, holding her hands up. "But it sounds like you could do with a drink."

Deborah said nothing as she watched the woman leave.

She'd been coming to this hall for almost a month now. Almost every time, Janice had been there. She was much older than Deborah. She didn't know where she lived or what she did for work. Didn't know if she had a partner, a family. By all accounts, Deborah and Janice were strangers, but she couldn't remember the last time someone had been so kind.

"That woman's here again," John said as he took his seat opposite Deborah, throwing his head behind him.

"Who?" asked the man next to him. A new face. Someone Deborah didn't know.

"I don't know her damn name. Just that she showed up last time and wiped the floor with us."

"If you got your head out of your ass for five minutes, you'd know her name is Maggie," Janice said, reappearing with two beers. "And she's nice. Works up at the gas station."

Suddenly their conversation was broken apart by the static of an aging microphone and the energetic voice of someone who didn't look older than sixteen. As the kid covered the rules and introductions for anyone new, Deborah quietly thanked Janice for the drink, rearranged the grid of numbers and empty squares in front of her, took the dauber from her pocket and unscrewed the lid. Then the numbers began.

The first time Maggie won that night, John threw his dauber to the table with a scowl. The second time, he swore so loud he got a warning. On the third and final time, he walked out, screaming to everyone that the game was rigged, while Janice threw her head back and laughed, saying Maggie was a woman so filled with luck it must be in her blood.

THE WALK back to Waxwing Creek took Deborah almost an hour. She never drove, but often considered it. It was a vehicle he wouldn't recognize, but the risk of the road always outweighed aching legs. She saw the lights of the motel before she got there, carving its place among the trees. In front of her room stood a darkened figure.

For a moment, her heart stopped. How had he found her? What was she going to do? But then, the panic started to settle. The figure was wrong. Too big around the gut. It was Walt Crane, the motel's owner, arms crossed around his body and a look in his eyes that told her he was gearing up for a fight.

"And where have you been this fine evening?"

"I don't think that's any of your concern," Deborah bit back, the fear still settling in her veins. She took the key from her pocket, wondering how she was going to get past him.

"When you're staying on my property and not paying, I'd say it is my concern. Now tell me where you've been, Deborah. Or should I call you Lindsay?"

The name hit her like a fist. If it wasn't for the wall offering support, the warmth of it under her hand, she could have passed out. Could have thrown up all over Walt's shoes. It had been months since she'd heard someone call her by her real name, and she didn't like it.

"I— I don't know what you're talking about."

"Oh, give it up," he said, leaning toward her, arms still crossed. "Your face gave you away soon as I said it. Now, I don't know what shit you've got yourself wrapped up in, and quite frankly, I don't give a rat's ass. I just—"

"Did you tell him?"

"Well, would you look at that."

"Did you? Did you tell him?"

"I don't remember telling you it was a man who called." Walt smiled smugly, like it was the most power he'd experienced in his life. "If there's anything running a place like Waxwing Creek teaches you, it's that you stay out of other people's business. It does not bode well to go sniffing shit that ain't yours. But when it's my money tied up in that shit, when it's my business on the line... Questions gotta be asked." Anticipation settled. Shouting started from the room next to hers. "No, I did not tell him."

Deborah wheezed, struggled to inhale, stumbling as she let go of the stress and tension gathered in her knees. She placed the back of a hand to her head, shaking as she wiped its sweat on her jeans.

"But, Deborah. Lindsay. Whatever the fuck your name is. What I said to you last night still stands. If you don't pay what you owe me in 48 hours, and if you so much as think about leaving without paying, I will tell him everything. You hear me?"

At that, Walt moved away from the door, and she fumbled with her key, missing the lock three times before entering. As soon as she closed it, shut herself off from the world, the fear piled itself on her chest. She started crying, throwing herself around the room. She checked to make sure the curtains were fully shut, checked under the bed, in the closet, behind the door in the bathroom. She wanted to tear the place apart, inch by inch, to check whether he had been in her room.

Every time she moved past the mirror, she forced her eyes away from it, scared she'd see his face there again, or hear his voice telling her she should be making her own luck. The possibility of him closing in on where she was staying ate at her. A part of her wanted to run as far and fast as her legs would carry her. To get in the beat-up car she had outside and drive, leaving her debt, Walt, and the memories of Waxwing Creek behind.

But it was the thought of what Walt had said that made her stay. Waxwing Creek, for all its grime, had become a haven. A place outside of his radar. He'd stumbled across her trail, but if Walt was telling the truth, he'd been thrown off her scent. The safest thing for her to do was wait. So that's what she did. She turned on the TV and sat on the bed, calculating how many games of bingo she could afford, what her probability of winning was, and how many nights that would buy her, over and over again.

As she contemplated, a storm arrived in Hunt so vicious it made the news. The gutters filled up with so much dirty rain and leaves ripped from branches that Walt spent the next day doing repairs. For some, that storm was a nuisance. For others, it was biblical. For Deborah, it was the force to which she formulated a plan.

In the years after, she'd think back to that night, wondering if it was the strength of the weather that informed the extremity of her decisions. Whether the sound of rain beating itself against her room's window forced the violence into her bones.

It's in her blood.

She heard Janice's voice say it again.

It's in her blood.

This time, she swore she could hear her husband's hurried whispers.

By the time the night was over, Deborah had clarity. If she wanted to stay hidden in the spaces unknown to her husband, she knew she had to pay her debt at Waxwing Creek before moving on. To do that, she needed money, and fast. So she did what she'd done for the last month. She'd fall back on bingo, the thing that had saved her before. The thing that was unassuming and quiet. The place that introduced her to people like Maggie, who had luck running in their blood.

THE NEXT NIGHT, as numbers were called, heads were lowered, and hands moved to put daubers to paper, Deborah didn't play. Instead, she waited. While those players left disgruntled, in search of warm beds, alcohol, or the company of lost lovers, Deborah sat on a bench, watching from the dark, waiting for Maggie to appear with the winnings she knew she'd have.

As the second to last car heaved itself over the small bump that separated the bingo hall's entrance from the rest of Hunt, the only sound around the empty parking lot was the scrape of candy wrappers and paper with numbered boxes skittering along the ground. She enjoyed the quiet and lack of activity, grateful for the absence of humanity.

In her back pocket, Deborah felt the dollar bills burn. There was enough there to change everything. Enough for just one more night of bingo.

As she was wondering whether she'd missed her, or if tonight was the night Maggie hadn't turned up, the door to the hall swung open and the woman stood there. She was skinny, with large glasses that made her small eyes look smaller and dark hair that stopped neatly above her shoulders. As Deborah made her way to the entrance, she thought Maggie looked more like a teacher than someone who worked in a gas station. There was something stoic about her. Bold. Upright. More than that though, she was a woman who'd won more games of bingo in the last week than Deborah had in her entire life.

"You did well tonight." It was a punt, presuming she'd won, but she figured it a good opportunity to test whether the woman's luck was real.

"My goodness, you made me jump," Maggie said, hand clutched around her throat. "I know! I can't believe it. That's three nights in a row." Deborah noted the roll of bills she folded and placed in her handbag. She forced herself to ignore it, pushing the possibility away. *Be patient*, she told herself. *Play your cards right and you'll have weeks of that.*

"Are you okay?"

"I'm not sure," Deborah lied. "I was waiting for a pick-up, but it doesn't look like they're coming."

"Oh." Deborah heard the hesitation in Maggie's voice. The way her eyes took her in, working while her mouth waited, open, to make an offer. "Well, do you need a ride somewhere?"

"Would you?"

"Of course," Maggie said. Deborah heard the confidence working its way back into the woman's voice, like saying it out loud made it more plausible. "Where are you headed?"

"Waxwing Creek."

"Waxwing Creek?" Maggie recoiled at the sound of it. "The motel? You're staying there?"

"If it's too much bother..."

"No, no, no. Don't be silly. It's no bother. My car's over there."

They walked together; Maggie in front, Deborah a step behind. Maggie kept herself busy with the car's keys, and Deborah kept quiet. She tried to come up with an alternative. A way out. But every time her conscience presented one, the sounds of the storm from the night before returned to eat it up and spit it out. Its rain reminded her of her husband. Its thunder turned into visions of him trailing her, smelling her out, whispering in her ear. In her mind, lightning struck suddenly, with violence, and she thought of him.

"Alright," Maggie muttered, sliding into the front seat. "Don't worry about that. Just move it into the back... That's right."

Deborah moved the papers before sitting in the passenger seat. The car was old but clean, the scented tree hanging from the mirror next to rosary beads doing nothing to smother its stale air.

"You ready?" Maggie said, fastening her seatbelt.

"I'm ready," Deborah said.

As Maggie craned her head to the back of the car to reverse out of her space in the parking lot, she caught Deborah's eye and smiled. Deborah knew it took a lot of trust to drive a stranger somewhere, especially when that somewhere was Waxwing Creek.

"So," Maggie said, straightening the wheel, "what brings you to bingo? Can't imagine it's the scenery. That hall needs more than a fresh lick of paint."

Deborah looked down. Nobody had ever asked her that.

"My husband."

"Oh? He's a regular?"

"No," Deborah said. "I haven't seen him in a while."

"Oh."

"A few months ago, I found out he was sleeping with another woman. Three other women, in fact. When I confronted him, he told me he was making his own luck. When I left, he tried to kill me. I've been on the run since."

"Goodness... I'm so sorry. I didn't mean to pry."

"You weren't prying."

"And that's why you're staying at Waxwing Creek?"

"That's why I'm staying at Waxwing Creek."

"Some people can be so cruel. There's a lot I want to say to you right now. To him too. But I'm gonna be honest. Bingo don't seem a place for someone who's on the run."

"My husband's an asshole, but he's smart. Persistent too. He's already checking the motels. He'll have his bases covered. Bingo's low profile. Easy. I never heard him mention it. And I guess I've come to like the luck of it. Every time a bill's due, I seem to get a win. Gives me faith that someone's got my back."

"Sweetie. Well, have you told anyone about this? Called the police?"

"I... I'm sorry."

"What's the matter? Are you alright?"

"Would you mind pulling over? I think I'm going to be sick."

Deborah had already checked the road in front and behind. She already knew it was the longest stretch between the bingo hall and Waxwing Creek. All that separated her and the rest of her life was going to happen now, on this endless plain of tarmac, surrounded by dense woods on either side.

As Maggie eased the car to a stop, Deborah didn't question what she was about to do. As she wrapped her hands around the woman's neck and squeezed harder than she'd ever squeezed anything in her life, she didn't second guess her decision. All Deborah thought about, as disbelief drained from Maggie's eyes and the woman's body spluttered and kicked, was that she was no different from her husband. Deborah imagined him watching. Smiling. Clapping.

Proud that she was finally making her own luck.

"I ALWAYS KNEW you had it in you."

The sound of his voice filled Deborah's ears. She turned, expecting to see his face, a gun in his hand. But the car was empty, save for her and Maggie, the woman she'd just killed.

She checked the mirror again, the beating of her heart lodged in her throat. She opened her door, rushing to push herself out of the car. With no headlights in front or behind, she placed both hands around the woman's shirt collar and, with one foot on the car as leverage, attempted to pull her across the vehicle. On the second pull, she noticed the woman was still strapped in, her hand twisted around the belt's buckle. Cursing to herself, she fumbled to unclip it before trying again, forcing herself to stop her hands from shaking. This time it worked, and she felt queasy at the feeling of Maggie's warmth on her skin and the heaviness with which the body slumped out of the car onto the side of the road.

She popped the trunk. It was empty, save for a carton of engine oil, which she moved to the side. After checking the road again, she grabbed Maggie's wrists, gritting her teeth as she dragged the corpse across the dirt to the back of the vehicle. It left a mark on the ground that looked like a tire had lost its grip. Not wanting to wait any longer, she used her adrenaline to muster every ounce of strength she had to pick up the body and place it in the back of the car. By the time she'd slammed the trunk shut and was back in the driver's seat, she was out of breath.

It hit her then how real Maggie was. The mirror was

wrong, the seat too far forward. With hands tight around the steering wheel, still warm from the woman's touch, she let the tears spill onto her cheeks and down her face, shaking in her seat.

Suddenly, a pair of headlights split the windscreen. She held her breath until the car passed.

She shifted into drive and pulled onto the road, still thinking of him.

There was a reason she was holed up in some shitty motel, with no money, no reason to live, killing people to try and improve her luck. This was his fault. *He* had forced her into this.

Soon, the glow of Waxwing Creek emerged in front of her, its lights particularly pretty as they reflected off the forest's leaves. She slowed the car to a crawl, taking stock of who was there, anxious at the possibility of seeing Walt Crane standing outside her door. She was relieved to see he wasn't. None of the rooms had people entering or exiting, and the office, which Walt usually sat in, was closed with wooden blinds covering the windows. As far as she could tell, the motel was asleep.

She backed the car into the space next to her station wagon, ensuring the trunk was as close to the door as possible. She killed the engine, and the quiet of the place settled around her.

She took the time to plan and take stock, to figure out how she was going to get the body cooling in the trunk into her room. Finally, she decided on sheets. She'd run into the room, grab the ones she needed from her bed, wrap up the body and bring it in. If anybody asked what she was carrying? Well, she'd worry about that then.

But nobody emerged. Not one soul set eyes on Deborah as she hurried to unlock the door of her room. Nobody witnessed her straining under Maggie's weight as she ambled into Waxwing Creek with a cadaver wrapped in cheap polyester. That night, there wasn't one witness.

So she didn't know if it was the panic of thinking she'd heard the door of another room open or the way her foot caught on the frame as she made her way in that made her drop the body, but the result was the same. It slipped out of her hands. The sound was thick, a dull crack as Maggie's skull hit the wall.

"Shit," Deborah whispered, closing the door and dropping to her knees. She saw the woman's shoulder touching the carpet, but her head hadn't quite made it. It was at an angle, pushed up against the skirting board. Blood bloomed on the bedsheets, turning them a deep red. Deborah scrambled into the bathroom, emptying the small trashcan of used tissues and empty travel-sized shampoo bottles onto the floor. When she returned, she tore the fabric from the corpse, lifting Maggie's head—just a little—so she could fit the trashcan under it.

She heard the change, the sound of drops making small, wet slaps as they hit the metal.

"That's it. Good girl. You'll want every drop."

She screamed at her husband, turning toward the bathroom mirror to see if his smiling face would be there. When she was confident that Maggie's blood was gathering in the trash can, she looked around for towels, clothes, anything to soak up what may stain the carpet.

As she searched, she returned to the bathroom and the razor caught her eye. She'd never had the courage to split her own skin, but figured she might be able to do it to someone else. She knew how to do it. She knew where to cut to get the most blood. She heard his voice again, telling her she could do it. Just one cut and it would all be hers. She removed the rusted blade from its holder, then rearranged the trashcan so it would catch what she needed. From the bathroom behind her, she heard the sound of her husband laughing.

In her room at Waxwing Creek, she got to work.

As Deborah walked into bingo the next evening, the others greeted her warmly. She returned the kindness, wondering whether they knew what her smile was hiding.

Walt Crane had given her until midnight, and she intended to pay the debt in full. If tonight's bingo session went as planned, if she got the wins she was hoping for, she'd be able to settle up and have a little left for the road. She'd already gotten rid of the body and the car, at least until she could get away. Deborah was so sure of her plan that, when preparing the corpse the night before, she'd stumbled across the purse Maggie had slipped her winnings into and decided to leave it in the woman's pocket. Deborah killed, but she didn't steal.

"Looks like Maggie's a no-show," Janice announced, bringing Deborah's thoughts back into the room. She swiveled her head to look around, playing along. Of course Maggie was a no-show. Then Deborah looked down, busying herself with her pad of numbers.

John, who'd made a guilty return, said, "Finally, some hope for the rest of us."

And then the numbers came with too much enthusiasm from a microphone that needed its wires replaced. The more Deborah placed her dauber to paper, the more she felt alive. The more she drenched the paper in liquid, the more certain she was that she'd done the right thing. Last night, she'd killed someone. She'd wrapped her fingers around a woman's throat and squeezed until the life was gone.

And this was why.

When Deborah shouted "bingo" to a room of strangers, she knew, with absolute certainty, that it was all worth it. For a fleeting moment, her husband didn't have control. He didn't exist. All that held her was elation. The body. The blood. The butchering. It was all, for a moment, worth it.

"Well, would you look at that," Janice beamed, grabbing Deborah's shoulder like they were best friends. "A full house."

"Must be that new dauber of hers," John said, nodding lazily toward her pad. "You don't see many using red."

THE MECHANIC

1998

Trey had been tracking the Mechanic for weeks. Been working to get in the same room as him so he could put a bullet in the man's head. Tonight, if he played his cards right, kept his cool, he was confident he'd be one step closer to making it happen.

The bar looked bleak, but it felt alive. Roseland, they called it. A dive in the center of Hunt with a reputation for being deadly. On either side of him, the bar ached under the weight of drunk elbows, and his ears rang from the rowdy shouts of people looking for their next hit. Behind him, a group of people huddled around hunched shoulders and hushed voices. In front, a neon sign with two crossed roses hung behind the bartender so bright it painted her silhouette red.

But no matter the company around him, the danger that loaded their words, Trey kept his focus on the man leaning over the bar to talk to him.

"You too?" Trey took note of the way the stranger lowered his voice. He'd seen how the man's face had changed when he'd mentioned the Mechanic. It was a risk, slipping it into conversation like that. It could've torn every-thing he'd worked toward apart. But the look the man gave Trey was worth it. The risk had paid off.

Trey leaned across the bar to meet him, trying to avoid the smell of alcohol and decay coming from the stranger's mouth.

"Me too," Trey murmured.

"Fuck, man. There's more of us out there than you think."

"I guess so."

"Hey, you want a drink?"

"Sure," Trey said. At this point, he knew his best hope—perhaps his only hope—was to get friendly with this guy. To act dirty and blend in. It hadn't been easy getting to this point, and he wasn't about to throw it away.

He watched the man raise his hand to the woman behind the bar, noting how loose the watch hung around his skinny wrist and how his eyes ate her up as she turned away. If things went south, he was confident he'd be able to take the man, with or without the help of the gun in his jacket.

When the woman returned, placing two pints in front of them, the man thanked her with a wink and suggested they take a seat in the empty booth behind them. As they did, he smiled. It lifted his thick, wiry eyebrows and accen-tuated the broken bones in his nose. His clothes, a plain t-shirt and battered work jeans, were well-worn, and he had a small scar running up the left side of his neck.

"So, what's your favorite?" Trey heard the excitement in his voice.

"My favorite?"

"From the movies," he said. "You know."

Trey guessed a question like this might come up, and he

had spent the last weeks watching as many horror movies as he could in the event he got quizzed on it.

"*Apex Horror* is pretty good for it," Trey said.

"You've got taste, man. The way she shakes the car, and she's crying and shit?" Trey could tell the man was getting into it. He sounded aroused, and Trey had to force his fingers from putting an end to him right there and then.

"Hey," the man said, urging Trey to lean in closer. "You wanna know something?"

"Sure."

"Next week will be my second time." Trey watched the corners of the man's mouth reveal rows of broken teeth. "Been saving for months. Never thought I'd be able to do it again. You should come see it."

Trey laughed. He didn't know if it was out of nervousness, fear, or the victory of being a step closer to the Mechanic.

"All right."

"Good," the man said, nodding vigorously. "That's good. Say, what's your name?"

"Javier," Trey lied.

"Javier," the man said, filling the holes in his teeth with a deep sip from his bottle. "Well, Javier. My name's Don, and I'm convinced you're about to see something you won't soon forget."

When the police officer told Trey his brother's death was gang-related, he hadn't believed him. When the officer stuck to his conclusion that he'd been caught in a crossfire of his own making, Trey had felt his fist aching for contact with the man's face. If the man hadn't been wearing a uniform or didn't have a standard-issue pistol strapped to his belt, Trey was sure he would have sucker-punched him. Take away the fact he was a cop, and Trey may have killed him.

Granted, his brother had fallen in with the wrong crowd. He'd witnessed it happen. Experienced the worry of seeing him disappear for weeks at a time. Rather than stop it, Trey had been there to pick up the pieces. He'd driven around their neighborhood looking for the silhouette of a man slumped in a back alley, stopping at crowds gathered around street corners to show his brother's photo.

But he'd heard how the bullet had landed. He'd gotten one of the cops so drunk he'd told Trey about the car's tampered wiring. "We put it down to gang violence," he'd said, the alcohol swelling his words. "*Always* put it down to gang violence. Less paperwork."

Naturally, getting to the truth had taken a lot of time. A lot of luck. A lot of conversations in places like Roseland with people he didn't like. As he lay looking at the unfamiliar ceiling of the house he was staying in, waiting for midnight, the dirty plates from dinner kicking up a smell at his side, he fixated on the look Don had given him when he'd slipped the Mechanic's name into the conversation. That look was one of reward: proof of how far he'd come.

Trey pushed himself up off the bed, aware he didn't have long to get where Don had said to meet him. He grabbed his jacket and the pistol from the bedside table, and reversed his car out of the house's front drive with a nervousness tugging at his insides.

He made his way back to Roseland, using it as a starting point to navigate his way out of Hunt. It took two hours before he rounded the car onto Alberta Avenue, following the directions Don had given him. He parked his car outside an abandoned office building, checked to make sure his vehicle was locked, and made his way across the street.

Hands in his pockets, head down, he turned his walk into a jog, moving away from Alberta Avenue until he met the most rundown block of apartments he'd ever seen. It was as though the place had slipped through a crack and been left to rot, alone, with no one to care for it. The buildings were tired, their sides supported by walls of built-up trash.

He found a bench, one of the planks missing from its bottom, and perched on its edge.

Then he saw the car. Don had said it would be there, and it was, the license plate matching the ink Don had scratched onto paper with a shaking hand. Its color was as nondescript as the accommodation beside it. Its side was dented, with battered and bruised paint.

Trey pulled his jacket around him, wondering where the strange man was.

It took 20 minutes for the building's door to open. All that time, Trey had been trying to untangle his fight or flight, steady the pendulum swinging from guilty to just. Imagining what was about to happen made him complicit. An accessory to a crime. But if it happened, it meant he'd be on the money; he'd know that Don was dealing directly with the Mechanic.

From the dark, Trey watched the woman head for the car, wondering where she'd be going so late. As she moved between streetlight and darkness, he did all he could to bite his tongue. He had the power to stop her from dying. Her fate rested in his hands.

She unlocked the vehicle, throwing her bag onto the passenger seat before slipping inside. Its door closed with a slam, and only the sounds Trey had been waiting for filled the air. As soon as the car refused to start and he heard the engine attempting to turn over, he could have cried. The industrial sound of metal on metal, brutal and euphoric, sadistic and sweet. Thoughts of his brother attached themselves to those sounds, sticking him to the bench. Memories stopped Trey from moving.

Had his brother tried as many times? Had the engine sounded the same when he turned the key over and over?

The lights of another vehicle parked down the street blazed to life, their beams pointing toward the woman like creatures on the hunt. As it pulled up beside her, its engine purring in defiance, Trey hoped it wasn't Don at the wheel. As a strange man pulled himself out of the car, using thin limbs to lift his skeletal body from the seat, Trey hoped it wasn't him. But he knew better.

Don made his way to the front of the hood. He took out a pistol and pointed it at the woman. Trey covered his mouth with the back of his hand, sinking his teeth into skin to hold himself together.

He watched Don wave the pistol's barrel around his head, toying with her, threatening her, getting his money's worth.

Panicked screams pierced the night. Trey saw her slapping a hand against the steering wheel while the other turned the key, forcing the car to continue yelling its own metallic panic.

And then it was done. The bullet travelled through the vehicle's windshield into the woman's face. The screams silenced, the car stopped shaking, and Don was rewarded with blood.

Trey ran. Fled the scene. Fell into his car, hands sweating, forcing the bile back down his neck. He drove as fast as he'd ever driven in his life, running red lights and accelerating on corners, until he was back at the house where the room was dark and a pillow was waiting to catch the yell lodged in his throat.

In Hunt, nothing had changed. Revelers still filled the bar. Lights still soaked the bar red. But the world felt different.

Last night, Trey had become a voyeur to a darker side of humanity. Now, the new world he navigated came with a hideous tint.

He grabbed a drink from the same woman who'd been working before and sat in the same booth he'd sat in with Don. Soon, Don arrived, and once more, Trey had to stop the bile rising in his throat.

"Javier." Don grinned, tapping the bottom of his bottle against the top of Trey's as he took a seat.

"Don," Trey said. He forced a weak smile, feeling the weight of the bottle in his hands, the gun in his inner pocket. He imagined the sensation of smashing the bottle into the man's face. He thought of how good it would look seeing his own face reflected in glass shards embedded in Don's skull.

"So?"

"I saw it," Trey murmured, taking a long sip of beer.

Don laughed, reaching a limb over the table to slap Trey hard on the shoulder. "I told you, man. He's the real fucking deal. Ain't no one in this town, hell, the world, who'll let you do something like that and clean up the mess after."

"I'll bet."

"Worth every cent, man. Every *fucking* cent. You know, when I left, I was worried you might've been a cop or something. But then I thought—there's no fucking way. They ain't smart enough to track down a guy like that. Would've put a stop to what he was doing a long time ago."

"I'm not a cop."

"I know, I know. So, tell me about it. How did it look?"

"It looked good," Trey lied. "I liked it."

"Gave you the taste you were after, huh? Make you want to experience the real thing?"

Trey looked at the man. Tried to see past the disgust to the soul buried underneath. He wondered what had to happen to someone to push them to such a dark place. At what point does someone become so damaged?

"Yeah," Trey said, forcing conviction into the way he nodded his head. "I think I'm ready to meet him."

Don locked eyes with Trey. He didn't know if it was what he'd seen the night before, or a change that came directly from Don, but something in his eyes seemed different. Whatever defined his vision before had left to make room for opportunity.

"You really want to go through with this?"

"I do."

"You got the money to make it worth his while? Mine too?"

"I do."

Don leaned back in his seat, biting his bottom lip with the few teeth he had left.

"There's a place on the other side of town. Waxwing Creek. If you're serious—if you really want this—you'll be there tomorrow. 10pm. Room five. No messing around."

"All right," Trey said.

"You've got no idea what I'm risking here, Javier. Do *not* be fucking late."

And with that, Don stood up, placed the empty bottle

on the bar, and stepped out, leaving Roseland's red for the rain.

Given its reputation, Waxwing Creek wasn't hard to find. He stared at the closed door of room five from his vehicle, wondering if it would be the last door he'd ever walk through. Taking a deep breath, he killed the engine, taking care to lock the car behind him. He noted the expanse of forest around the motel. Not even a hint of wind stirred the leaves.

The motel appeared empty. Nobody exited or entered rooms, no lights shone in the windows. Fitting, he thought, if he was about to meet his end. He approached room five and knocked, listening to something shuffle behind the door. It opened and Don offered a meek smile, motioning Trey inside.

The room was bleak, with a made bed, a cigarette-burned table, and a lone chair tucked into the corner. The walls contained questionable stains, and part of the carpet was torn. He started to understand why the place had such a reputation.

"Where is he?" Trey asked.

"Who?"

"The Mechanic."

Don laughed, head thrown back. "It don't work like that, man." Trey felt uncertainty, and it was making him nervous.

"Well, how does it work?"

"You make me an offer, and I tell you if it's worth my while."

"I'm pretty new to this," Trey said. "I wouldn't wanna lowball you."

Don put his hand up, motioning Trey to be quiet.

"You know much about this place?" Don asked, taking a cigarette out of his shirt pocket.

"The motel?"

Don grunted, lighting it with cupped hands and urgent puffs.

"Not much."

"You're not from around here, huh? If you were, you would've heard about it. Built on top of a house where a family was murdered. Killed in cold blood. The first owners just bulldozed in, knocked it down, and built Waxwing Creek in its place. Now they say it's haunted by that family," Don said, pointing a lazy finger at him. "Ghosts, Javier. Real fucking ghosts. Talk about a rough start, huh?"

"Right," Trey muttered.

"But you know what? I like it here. It always felt like home. Waxwing Creek holds a special place in my cold, old heart." Don chuckled, patting the flat of his palm against his chest. "And why wouldn't it? This is where I heard about the Mechanic. They told me all about him, Javier."

"Who did?"

"The ghosts. I'm telling you. All the stories you hear about this place? All the horror people think is trapped in its walls? It's all real. But I'm an optimist. I approached it different. This place was my gateway to euphoria. You understand that? My path to him was paved with the words I heard in this very room. That's why I wanted us to meet here. Just us. This motel changed my fucking life, man. And I believe it will change yours too."

"That so?" Trey got the sense Don was trying to connect with him. Trying to find common ground. He didn't believe what he was saying, but he felt uneasy. He was counting down the seconds to get out.

"I ever tell you about my first kill? Some poor soul out in Riley Falls."

"Riley Falls?" Trey almost choked on it. He felt the dread wash over his body, letting its coldness trickle from his neck, down his spine, across every hair on his body.

"You know it?"

"Yeah," Trey said, struggling to push the words past the possibility.

"How?"

"Dated a girl out that way," he lied.

"Lucky bastard." Don laughed. "Bet she fucked like a dog, huh? Women from those towns always do."

"Yeah." Trey laughed. He felt his muscles aching as he released the tension in his fists. Around him, the motel felt heavy. Its walls overbearing, like the establishment was releasing a persistent, grating hum.

"Well, you're in the clear then. It was some dropout. Mechanic's smart like that. Always picks the ones on drugs. The forgotten. Ones who won't be missed."

"Did you know their name?" Trey didn't want to ask. He didn't want the answer. He thought of all the nights he'd spent looking for his brother, lost after another high. He thought about whether he was so far gone the Mechanic had deemed him "forgotten."

"I don't remember," Don said, face contorted as he emptied smoke from his lungs. "Can you believe that? My first one, and I'm struggling to remember. Saw the police report the next day though. Couldn't fucking believe it. Pigs put it down to gang violence."

THE SOUND of the bar swelled around him, replacing thoughts of his brother and blood with drunken shouts and the sound of glass on glass.

"Did you hear what I said, man?"

"I heard you," Trey replied. "'Don't say anything about mechanics.'"

"I mean it. This shit wasn't easy. You've got one shot at this. Do not fuck it up."

Trey didn't like how anxious Don was. He didn't like how much the man's bones twitched. He'd come to Hunt to put a bullet in the Mechanic. After their conversation at Waxwing Creek, that bullet had turned to two.

"Then why didn't we meet somewhere quieter? Why didn't we meet at the motel?"

"Because he don't work like that. He wants places busy."

Trey looked around, wondering if anyone else had done business with the Mechanic, exchanging cash, earned or stolen, for a couple minutes in a twisted heaven. He wondered if the Mechanic was already here, listening in on their conversation, watching their every move. A nervousness slipped up his vertebrae. A dampness started to seep from his palms. Suddenly, the gun resting in his pocket felt heavier and the room's atmosphere more menacing. The Mechanic was close. So close.

"What did you tell him?" Trey said.

"What?"

"What did you tell him? About me?"

"What do you fucking think I told him? Said you got a kick out of seeing people panicking in cars that won't start. That you wanted the thrill of being the bad guy, like in the movies. Now will you chill the fuck out?"

Trey hunched his shoulders, looking into his drink. He

tried to level his breathing, steady his stomach, going back over the route he'd take to the nearest exit one more time.

"That's him," Don mumbled, offering a curt nod over Trey's shoulder. "I mean it. Do *not* mention mechanics."

Trey had heard about hiding in plain sight, but when an elderly man with a rough plaid shirt tucked into battered jeans, wearing a cap with tufts of hair sticking out its sides sat opposite him, Trey couldn't help but release a dry laugh. The Mechanic had a thick mustache that sat below wide glasses, and Trey could smell his chewing gum. Beside him, he felt Don stiffen. In front of him, the Mechanic had a look in his eyes that challenged Trey to laugh again.

Trey's back started to sweat. His insides squirmed. He could hear his heartbeat in his ears, and his fingers itching for the trigger.

"This him?" The Mechanic's voice sounded tired. Weathered. Old and more fragile than Trey had imagined.

"It's him," Don said. "Man, it's so great to see you again. I'm telling you—"

"And the money?"

"Don't worry," Trey reassured him, reaching into his pocket. "I've got enough for you both."

FIVE MINUTES

2007

THEY'D AGREED to meet on the third floor of London's Royal Hotel. As Henry Merville readied himself for what was about to happen, outside the night sky released a gentle rain.

He checked his watch. Two minutes.

Assessing his appearance in the bathroom mirror, Henry tilted his head to the side. He admired the short facial hair trimmed around a handlebar mustache that sat below small circular glasses, and he had grown a fondness for the wrinkles around his mouth and eyes. He liked the way his suit looked in this light: the depth of hue that high-lighted the tailoring, the patterned handkerchief sticking a corner out of the breast pocket. It all assembled well.

When the knock arrived, he patted down the crisp creases in his suit trousers one final time, breathed deep, and opened the door.

"Mr. Davis," he said, filling his face with a smile. "It's a pleasure. Come in, come in. Isn't the weather just ghastly?"

Mr. Davis was dressed in a white button-up shirt and dark denim jeans, with shoes that shone like the puddles outside. He had clearly made an effort. The clothes were clean, the hair freshly trimmed, and Henry couldn't help but notice the strength of cologne as he passed him.

"Here, let me take your jacket," Henry said. Mr. Davis passed it over, fiddling nervously with his shirt collar as he walked to the other end of the room. Henry hung the jacket in the wardrobe, noting the wet patches that stained the pits and the effort the man made to avoid eye contact.

"The payment," Mr. Davis said.

"Oh no, no. Don't worry about that. Let's focus on setting the mood. Getting things right. Did it take you long to get here?"

"Not really. I live on the other side of the city, but I ended up taking a cab."

"Excellent. I can't begin to imagine how difficult the last months have been for you. A death is never easy, no less when it's someone you love. You have my condolences."

Mr. Davis said nothing. Instead, he swayed from heel to heel in the room's corner.

"Mr. Davis," Henry said, sweeping back to check the door lock. "I can sense you are nervous, and that is understandable. Indeed, this is an unusual situation. But in order to ensure the best results, you must try to calm yourself. I assure you, there is nothing to worry about. Please," Henry motioned to the bed, "take a seat."

Henry made sure to continue smiling while Mr. Davis perched on the edge of the bed.

"Good." He made his way back to the room's dark wooden desk, where he'd set aside two champagne glasses beside an open bottle. "Now. The key to making this night a success lies in this bottle." As he said it, he started filling the two glasses, lifting one to the light to peer through the golden liquid. "You'll notice it's flat, but that's how I like it.

There's something about the effervescence that pulls me out of the mood."

"What do you mean?"

Henry paused to look over his shoulder, offering an understanding smile.

"I work better without bubbles." Henry lifted the glasses from the desk, gliding over to the bed. "Cheers," he said, handing its long stem to the stranger.

"Cheers," Mr. Davis said.

Henry watched as the man tipped the glass and emptied the liquid into his mouth.

"Fabulous," Henry said, returning the empty glasses to the desk and then positioning the desk's chair in front of where Mr. Davis was sitting. "Now, I'm going to explain what will happen here, and I want you to listen very carefully. There's a lot that goes into this. A lot that...coalesces. To ensure this goes smoothly—seamlessly—your co-operation is required."

"Okay," Mr. Davis said.

"But before we go any further, I want to ask—and know that I ask this of all my clients—are you sure you want to go through with this?"

"I'm sure."

It was the surest Henry had seen Mr. Davis since he'd entered. He believed him and took comfort from it. If there was anything he didn't want to do, it was start the process with someone who wasn't committed.

"Good. Now, there are three things you should remember. First: everything that happens here tonight will take place in this room and will *stay* in this room. I won't tell a soul, and I encourage you to do the same. Second: I don't know how long it will take for me to bring your wife back. Sometimes, it takes an hour. Other times, a matter of minutes. All I ask is that you remain patient, vigilant, and do not disturb me during the process. Rest assured that she will know of tonight's intentions before she arrives. You don't have to spend any time explaining. Any questions so far?"

"No. No questions."

"Third: when she arrives, I will leave the room. Give you both some privacy. From that moment, you'll have five minutes. Not a second more. Not a second less. After those five minutes, you won't see me again. You'll leave the hotel the same way you entered. You don't need to worry about cleaning up, and you don't need to send me a note of thanks. As far as you are concerned, the moment this interaction ends, I do not exist. I am *not* in the business of repeat business, Mr. Davis. Understood?"

"Understood. But..."

"Yes?"

"I do have one question. When we're, you know. When we're doing it, do I have to wear anything?"

"A condom, you mean? Mr. Davis, that is personal preference, though I would advise you do so merely for the sake of clean up."

"Right. And how will I know when she's here?"

"Oh, you'll know. But like I said, there is nothing to worry about. She will know what you intend to do before she arrives. If, for any reason, your wife refuses your advances, I will call off the meeting immediately. Your safety, and her safety, are my top priorities. Is that all?"

"I have another question."

"What's that?"

"Why are you not in the business of repeat business?"

Henry looked into the man's eyes. He noted the glimmer of hope, fighting through the defeat. Saw how desperately hard the last weeks had been for him and felt himself soften. He'd never been asked that before. Never given someone the chance. Taking a moment to consider how far he'd come, he questioned how many lives he could have saved, or destroyed, by offering his services.

"When you feel your wife's presence enter this room, you'll sense something so profound and powerful that it will scare and thrill you in equal measure. You will, I suspect, hate that you are here, but you will also thrive on the knowledge that you could do it again. You'll see in it the dangerous potential for addiction."

"Right."

"Mr. Davis, you need to understand that what we are about to do here is out of this world. It is supernatural. Unfathomable. To the majority, unbelievable. While some engage my services for a final conversation or to seek some sort of closure, you have chosen to spend your five minutes making love to your wife one last time. Regardless of the reason, my work deeply and irreparably breaks the rules of being alive. I don't believe it is good for any person, living or dead, to have to break those rules more than once. Now, is that all?"

"Yes, yes," Mr. Davis said, a sheepish look on his face. "That's all."

"Wonderful." Henry clapped both hands to his skinny knees, leaning forward with a satisfied smile. "Mr. Davis, if you are ready, we can begin."

As HENRY SAT at the desk of his loft apartment, he thought about that night with Mr. Davis, how successful it had been.

It took him back to the first night he realized he could interact with the dead.

He'd been eating dinner with a woman named Claire. She'd lost her wife, Julia, two weeks before when part of a bus stop bench had punctured her left lung. The coroner had ruled her death a car accident, and a textbook one at that. The real cause of death, as Henry would find out that evening, wasn't the metal from which the paramedics had to remove her from, but the bright sign placed in front of a church she'd leaned forward to read moments before.

The funeral had been short, the grief so uncontrollable it felt violent, but Claire climbed out of it and, whether as an act of courage or defiance, invited her closest friend to dinner.

"Oh, Henry, I'm so glad you're here," she'd said, using a cloth to transfer hot plates to the table.

Henry had raised his glass and toasted her. "And I'm so glad you survived."

The room had been filled with the scent of baked fish, and his fingers had smelt of lemon when Claire's late wife had entered Henry's orbit.

Whenever he thought back to what it felt like, the only word he could muster was *damp*. It was as though TV static, cold and wet, had slipped itself into the spaces that separated skin and bone, invading his entire being. It wasn't a substance or anything Henry could grasp, but a feeling. An idea he couldn't quite formulate. A realization that someone he knew was present.

That first time, Henry had gripped the edge of the table, wondering whether he was having an allergic reaction to the fish or a panic attack so profound it was making him hallucinate. The room had spun and food had somersaulted in his belly. As it did, all he'd felt was that cold wetness creeping up his spine and into his neck, more intense, more profound than anything he'd ever experienced, bringing with it an urge to run to the bathroom and vomit.

Then he sensed the static turn to substance. First it was slow, but the more he acknowledged it, the greater the slime hardened. He felt Julia not just in his orbit, but *as* his orbit. They were circling each other, moving together in one brilliant, bizarre dance. The woman, who he'd known almost as long as he'd known Claire, was in his brain with him, moving with him, communicating with him, and he had no idea how to get her out.

All he felt was an overwhelming urge to open his mouth and tell Claire, on Julia's behalf, that everything was all right. That she would laugh at the way the church had killed her, letting her know it didn't want her after all. That she was fine. That Claire would, and should, move on.

But Henry never told Claire about the way her wife had died. He was too scared to share any supernatural encouragement for her to move on. When Henry finally forced himself back to stability and felt confident Julia had left his orbit, he had dabbed the corners of his mouth with the perfume-soaked napkin and made an excuse to leave.

Since then, the unexplained incidents continued. A strong shiver as he walked past a doorway. A state of queasiness as he rounded certain stairs. But every time the dead attempted their advances, and he'd feel their damp pushing on his brain, he'd shut them down, switch them off, and tell them to head the other way.

That was until a cold evening one February, when he was lying in a clawfoot tub. Slow jazz played on the radio as he made his way through a box of chocolates dusted with icing and a glass of disappointingly flat champagne. The day had been long and arduous, spent at the luxury restaurant where he worked behind the bar, mining dull conversations for something shiny.

The bath's water had been cooling to an uncomfortable temperature. He'd placed the flat champagne on the floor, leaning over to turn on the hot faucet, thinking back to Julia's presence under his skin, when he felt it again: the wet sensation pushing against his skull. He didn't know who or what it was, only that they were pushing him so hard that when he urged them to move back, tried to turn off his own internal tap to the spirit realm, they didn't listen.

Rather than continue the fight, he embraced it. He lay back so the bath's water covered his ears, let its dying warmth gather around his eyes, and allowed the dampness to take control.

He felt the presence of a man named Carmen enter his orbit. A man that urged him to sip the champagne. *"Take a drink,"* the dead man told him. *"It'll settle your nerves."* He drank, and it did. Then Carmen had urged him to not just take hold of his spirit, but to wrap his mind around him and pull as hard as he'd ever pulled anything in his life.

Henry did. He worked his thoughts around the man's essence, threading the motions of his mind through the man's memories, trying to get a grip on something that felt physical. Then he pulled as hard as he could, and in that pull, Henry knew he'd changed something. Broken something.

When he watched the water in the bath move itself around another body, invisible but physical, Henry understood the weight of what he'd accomplished. Then he'd felt Carmen's hand and saw the bath's faucet turn on its own.

Henry shook the thought away, replacing memories with the dark desk in front of him, sighing about the time that had passed since.

He opened his laptop, straining his eyes against the brightness. The ping of a new email signaled its arrival from Roger Jackson, a name he wasn't familiar with. He pushed his glasses farther up his nose and opened up the message to read.

"Christ," Henry muttered to himself. He stepped away from the laptop to the kitchen, where he poured himself a large glass of red wine. This wasn't the first time a stranger had reached out to him *"through a friend of a friend."* Most requests arrived by word of mouth. The thought of Roger Jackson's proposal made him anxious. The travel wasn't a problem, and the money was good, but he didn't like the idea of so many people knowing how he supported his income. Sighing to the empty room, he retook his seat and started typing.

Roger,

I believe you've reached the right person, though I would be interested in hearing who shared my contact information. In the meantime, you are welcome to send over the relevant details. Be clear but concise. I'll be in touch soon after.

Kindest regards,

Henry

The laptop let Henry know his message had been sent. He sat, lost in thoughts of past experiences, until the sound of a new email pulled him back to the screen.

Roger shared how he'd lost someone close to him—Stacey—five months ago, but he had fallen out with her family during their relationship. He'd been banned from the funeral, the grief, and wanted a chance to say goodbye properly. As Henry took another sip from his glass, one line from the email stared at him.

Name your price and I will pay it.

This was a man who was desperate, and Henry knew that where there was desperation, there was money.

If Stacey's family found out I was talking to you, they'd kill me, the email continued. *I've found a place that'll suit. It's quiet, in a town called Hunt. There'll be no trace we were ever there.*

"Hunt," Henry said aloud. He removed his glasses, closing his eyes to rub where the pads had been pressed into his nose. Henry tutted, as perplexed as he was impressed that his business had gone global. He crafted an email offering his condolences, telling Roger that he wasn't accustomed to leaving the country on business, but for the right price, he was willing to make an exception.

THE MAN in the taxi shouted at Henry, his accent thick.

"Where are you going, buddy?"

"Oh," Henry said, leaning toward the driver's open window. "Hunt. Please."

The driver paused, looking Henry up and down. He took in the loud suit, the neat mustache, and the small, round specs, letting his face scrunch into itself. "Where in Hunt?"

"Waxwing Creek. The motel."

"Waxwing Creek?"

"That's right. I've heard it's not far from here."

"It isn't far, but it isn't close either. You got enough money for a trip like that?"

"Oh, yes," Henry said. "Certainly."

"And if you don't mind me saying," the driver continued, "you don't look like a man destined for a place like Waxwing Creek. You sure you got the right place?"

"I'm sure," Henry said.

"Alright." The driver shrugged, hands in front of him. "Get in."

The driver hadn't been lying. It took almost an hour to get to Hunt, where everything felt different than the tightness he was used to back in London. They passed diners and dive bars, garages and gated properties. At one point, Henry had to shield his eyes against the bright neon of its bingo hall. Everything here felt alien. American. Through the entirety of the journey, the driver didn't say another word.

Eventually, Waxwing Creek grew out of the dark like a thrumming mass of fireflies. Henry noted the sign hanging out front, the metal a lighter color where it was missing one of its Ws.

Welcome to WAXING CREEK.

The taxi pulled up at the front, and Henry got out of the vehicle with a grunt.

"Thank you," Henry said, leaning over to pay the fare. Remembering where he was, he left a little more.

"You look after yourself, brother," the driver said, nodding toward the motel. "Heard a lot of bad shit about that place. A lot of stories. A lot of evil. The less time you're here, the better."

Henry turned to meet Waxwing Creek. He'd heard of American motels, set up at the edges of long and dusty highways, had even seen a few movies about them. From the outside, this one didn't look like the ones he'd seen on screen.

He'd looked it up before. He'd read the bad reviews. He knew about its legacy, which is why, when Roger Jackson insisted they meet at Waxwing Creek, he'd arranged to stay somewhere different. But none of that unsettled him. What unsettled him was the gentle hum of dampness that filled his head, the wetness pushing against his skull. He didn't need bad reviews or the warnings of a taxi driver to know there was evil lurking here.

As the taxi retreated behind him, he took in the surrounding forest, its depth thick like ink. As he approached and opened the door of the office on the building's left, he smelled the room's dilapidation, saw the desk made of plastic that looked like wood, and started to trust an intuition that told him this place had seen a lot of bad shit.

Before him sat a heavy-set man who looked tired and defeated, legs up on the desk, newspaper open in both hands. When Henry entered, the man stopped reading. Henry registered the way he took him in, navigating his eyes up and down what he was wearing.

"Can I help you?"

"I have a room booked here. For tonight."

"You're Patrick," he said, nodding, sharing the name Henry had given him. "Right?"

"Yes, I—"

"Since the day I took over Waxwing Creek, no son of a bitch has ever booked a room at this place a month in advance." The man laughed. "We get more of the impulse clientele, if you catch my drift."

"Quite," Henry murmured.

"Don't know what I was expecting, but you was certainly not it. Room three," the man shouted, swinging his legs to the floor, using his feet to drag the chair across the room's brittle carpet. "I've only got one key, but your friend's already in there."

"I'm sorry?" It came out of Henry like an offended outburst. Usually, he wanted time to prepare, to see where his work would be taking place. That's why he booked. He made that clear to every client.

"I said your friend, if that's what you wanna call him, is already in there, waiting to get going with whatever it is you two have planned." The man smirked. "We don't usually get your kind out here, in a small town like this. I'd watch yourself if I was you."

"Goodness," Henry murmured to himself. "Well, thank you for your kindness. Room three, you say?"

"Room three."

Henry left the room flustered, so irritated that Roger had arrived before him that he'd missed the man's comments. He walked toward the door emblazoned with a metal 3 and stopped a second, taking a moment to listen before knocking.

No sooner had he knocked than the door opened to whom he presumed was Roger Jackson. He looked different than what Henry expected. He'd imagined someone burly, in the later stages of life, but he was met with someone skinny and younger, with a sullen look around the eyes.

"Mr. Jackson?"

"Holy shit," the man said, ushering him inside. Henry could tell he was from America, but a different part. "You're actually here."

"Yes, yes, but Mr. Jackson, in my last email, I shared that I would arrive here early. Before you. That I would need some time alone. What we're doing here takes time to prepare, both mentally and physically."

Roger moved behind him to shut the door. Henry faltered, trying to shake away the uncertainty scratching at the periphery of his mind. The dampness here was pushing, hard.

"I know, I know," Roger said. "But I was just so excited to meet you, man. I wasn't expecting you to show up."

"Right," Henry murmured. One hand tightened its grip around his suitcase while the other rubbed his chin. "Well, if you don't mind, I still need some time to get ready. To compose myself. It's been a tiring day of travel, as I'm sure you understand."

"Oh, I understand. But I ain't going anywhere."

Henry's mind took him through all the clients he'd seen over the years, all the people he'd helped. He'd seen all spectrums of the human condition, from lust to fantasy to fear, but this was different. He didn't think this man was here longing after someone to say a final goodbye. This man wanted something more.

"Okay," Henry said, thinking carefully about his words and whether there was a way out. "On this occasion, I will make an exception. But I still need to get a few things in order. My suitcase. May I?"

"Sure," Roger said, nodding. Henry moved toward the bed and unzipped the case in one swift motion, flattening it out so it looked like an unhinged jaw. Inside lay a small collection of clothes Henry was hoping to travel around the area with after this appointment and a resealed bottle of champagne.

"I bought it at the airport," Henry said, answering the puzzled look on Roger's face. "Opened it there so it would lose its fizz. I need two glasses."

"Glasses? Waxwing Creek ain't that kind of place, man. There are plastic cups in the bathroom."

"Yes. Right."

Henry balked at the brightness of the bulb as it illuminated the tiny bathroom. He looked at himself in the mirror. Sweat beaded across his brow, and a twitch was kicking up a fuss under his eyelid. It always happened when he was stressed, and he willed it to quiet down. He carried the cups into the bedroom, offering Roger an awkward smile, then grabbed the champagne bottle from the suitcase, and set them all down on the table. All the while, Roger stared at him, following his movements through darkened eyes.

"Mr. Jackson, before we begin, I need to go over a few... guidelines with you," Henry said, cursing at the handful of bubbles pressing themselves from the bottom of the plastic cup. "Just to ensure the safety of you and Stacey."

"Alright." Roger shrugged.

"Here," he said, handing over the champagne. "Drink this. It will help set the mood. Put things in motion." He was surprised when Roger didn't complain or ask any questions. Instead, the man looked at the alcohol hungrily, tilted his chin and, without taking his eyes off Henry, tipped it back and drank it all.

"Lovely," Henry murmured, taking the cup back from him. "Would you be so kind as to take a seat? I know how anxious you must be. I would be too. But I'm feeling on edge about the situation. To achieve the best results tonight, we need to be calm, thorough. I'd appreciate it if you would sit with me while I explain what's going to happen."

The man sighed impatiently and sat at the room's small table.

Then Henry explained, as he did every time. He told Roger what to expect and what the ground rules were. Don't disturb while attempting to bring Stacey here. Their safety was his top priority. He told him about payment and not being in the business of repeat business. The routine of it, scripted and perfected over months of charging people to connect with the dead, made it easier.

And though he wasn't comfortable with it and though

the mood hadn't been set, the champagne wasn't flat, and he felt anxious, tired, and unprepared, he decided he was ready.

He traded places with Roger so that he now sat on the chair, and Roger sat on the bed. Then he closed his eyes, opened himself up to the damp pressure, and entered the unknown.

The feeling of it filled him so fully, he had to struggle to not lose himself. He'd traveled up and down England's countryside, visiting abandoned schools and forgotten landmarks, cemeteries, and other locations people thought would better connect him with their lost ones. In truth, Henry didn't need any of that. All he needed was the person who was looking. If they were close by, he'd have a compass.

But at Waxwing Creek, that felt different. So much energy and negativity were soaked into the motel's walls that Henry was having a hard time navigating it, and all the compass did was spin.

He focused, forcing himself to venture deeper, trying to use Roger as a guide. He allowed the damp to take control, wading through the trauma of the place, arms out as though he were swimming. He saw flashes of bingo lights and blood, a flurry of fingers clutched around a woman's neck. He saw racks of spines, hanging from mouths like long white tongues, and an eternal expanse of forest keeping watch. He saw a family piled like dirty laundry, dead in a cramped attic.

It was disturbing, all of it, but it wasn't what Henry was looking for. He searched again, swimming through the noise, trying to connect memory to memory, feeling to feeling, impulse to impulse, drawing on the presence of the strange man sitting beside him.

But every time he tried to push toward Stacey, the woman Roger was looking for, he met resistance. Every time he took another turn toward the woman Roger loved, he was met with blanks. So instead of waiting for the dead to push him, he pushed them. He searched them, holding onto what he knew of Stacey, of her connection to Roger, using the knowledge of others in the spirit realm to send him in the right direction.

Until, finally, he found her.

She was blurry and indistinct, like a window filled with condensation. He couldn't see what she looked like, only that there was something there moving, whirling. He invited her in, trying to coax her forward with the promise of meeting Roger, a man she loved. Still, he felt resistance. He felt the woman, and her spirit, pull back, and the vision in front of him filled with so much fog it turned to water. Water that throbbed so hard, it turned into a wave that jolted him out of his trance.

He was back at Waxwing Creek, unsuccessful, mentally bruised, sitting in a chair next to Roger Jackson.

"Well? Where is she?"

Roger's voice sounded loud and overbearing, like a gun had gone off. Henry answered the question by lifting his hands to cover his ears. He took a moment to take in his surroundings, adjusting to the dim light.

"Henry? Where is she, man?"

Henry looked at the stranger, taking in the desperation in his eyes, the tension in his stature. He understood the danger of what he was doing. In that man's stare, he saw the dark places this job could take him. In that moment, he vowed this would be his last job. When he left Waxwing Creek, he'd never take on another client again.

"Mr. Jackson, would you pass me some water?"

To Henry's continued surprise, the man listened, hurrying to the washroom, where he heard the faucet running. When he returned, Henry accepted the plastic cup, emptying it in a few large gulps.

"Well? Where's Stacey?"

"I–I–I don't know."

"What do you mean you don't know?"

"I made contact with her."

"But?"

"But she didn't want to make contact with you, Mr. Jackson. As far as I understand it, she refused to come through."

"What do you mean, refused?" Henry could tell his client was getting agitated.

"I asked her, invited her to come through. She refused. So, I think it's in our best interest if we cut this event short. Sometimes—"

When Roger pulled the gun from behind his back and pointed it at Henry's head, he felt fear so pronounced he almost wet himself. Henry had never seen a gun, let alone looked down the barrel of one. He stumbled over his own breath, pushing his back against the chair, struggling to release the words, screams, or whatever noise was trapped at the back of his throat.

"Don't move, and don't make a sound," Roger said. "Or I swear to God I'll blow your brains out."

Henry held up his hands. "Mr. Jackson," he finally said. "I–I–I–I don't know what you think this is."

"You said you found her. You said you spoke with her."

"Well," Henry said, swallowing his fear.

"That's what you just said!"

"Mr. Jackson. Roger. I said I made *contact* with her. You have to understand that communication doesn't happen there as it does here. You don't converse in the same way."

"I don't give a fuck what you do when you're there. I'm paying you to bring Stacey here, so I expect you to do that."

"Mr. Jackson," he pleaded, struggling to regain composure. "Please. You need to listen to me. The safety—"

"Try it again."

"Look."

"Try it *again!*" This time Roger shouted it, cocking the pistol for dramatic effect. The pair fell silent. The only sounds came from each of their breathing. Henry thought through his options. Thought through his death and what it would look like if this continued. Considered how he'd ended up here and how he was going to make it out alive. He'd never encountered a spirit that didn't want to come through, let alone attempted to bring someone here against their will. But with the gun pointed at him and his death a few wrong words away, he decided to dance with danger and outline the risks one last time.

"Mr. Jackson. I'm not trying to be difficult, but you have to hear what I am saying. You have to understand that what I do— It is not easy. We're talking about communicating with the dead here."

"I don't care if you're communicating with J.F. fucking K. I am paying for this, so I am going to get what I paid for. And if you don't, I will use this gun to paint these walls with your face."

Henry nodded, wiping the sweat from his palms on the legs of his trousers, working his tongue around his dry mouth. The inevitability was present and it was heavy. He was going to have to try it again.

"And don't think you can pretend," the man continued.

"I saw how your eyes changed when you was doing what you was doing. I'll know if you're back there."

Henry took a moment to settle himself, preparing for what was ahead.

"The champagne," Henry murmured, motioning toward the table. "Pour me another glass."

He watched Roger think about it, considering whether or not he should oblige. When the man declined with a shake of his head and a firm "nu uh," Henry cursed this motel. Cursed the moment he'd ever felt the presence of the dead swimming in his system with a belly full of fish and potatoes, and cursed this rotten part of the world. Gathering his composure, trying to suppress the danger he could face by reentering unprepared, he closed his eyes.

Then, he was back.

The realm of the dead felt different, as though he wasn't welcome anymore. The fog that typically shrouded him from a person shrouded him from everything. It was like all the souls it was holding had coalesced into one heaving, moving mass of gray that he was going to struggle to break through. Knowing his life depended on it, he pushed on. He forced himself to break through it, knowing if his task here didn't end in success, he, too, would become part of its thickness.

He moved as he did before, using Roger's energy to direct him. He slipped from one pulse to the next, each with a different strength, until eventually, he entered Stacey's orbit.

Last time, she'd been encased behind a layer of mist so thick he couldn't see through it. The mist was there, but now it was thicker, louder. He moved toward it, feeding off its vibrations to muster the strength to push him closer to it.

The mist dissolved quicker than Henry could process it,

and through its thickness emerged a face split open in the middle, with pieces of blood and bone pouring from its center and an eye severed in half. Henry felt his senses recoil, horrified by the images. Here, he didn't just see the wound but felt it, as if it was his own face that had split, with his own bones splintered and spread through the gore.

As he tried to take it in and attempted to make sense of what was happening, Stacey's voice reached him. It sounded clear but unclear, smothered in smoke and static.

"He did this to me!" She screamed it. Throttled him with it. *"That piece of shit did this to me. He put me here. He killed me in this motel."* As much as Henry wanted to, he couldn't look away. Icy fingers forced him to watch, keeping his head steady and his eyelids open, making him see what the monster sitting next to him in the motel room was capable of.

Before he had a chance to respond, they kicked him out. Thrust him from their home with such force he landed back on the chair at Waxwing Creek so hard he felt every fiber in his body spasm.

"Henry?" That voice again. Roger's. "Henry? Talk to me, man."

Henry kept his head lowered. His eyes stung and his head was pounding. His mouth tasted of blood. He knew he had a choice, but his mind was already made up. For years he'd been seeking the company of the dead, uninvited. He'd pushed himself into their home, their peace, and given them a glimpse of what it would be like to return.

Today, he'd seen that it didn't just lead to trauma, but that he was, in fact, unwelcome. So when Roger prompted him to speak—to open his fucking mouth and talk—he said what he said for the woman he'd met in the fog. He said it for Stacey.

"I know why she won't come back," Henry murmured, pursing his lips to muster enough saliva to whisk the words together.

"What did you say?" Roger spat the words at him.

"I said I know why she won't come back." Henry forced his head up, locking eyes with a man he now knew was a killer. "You took that woman's life. You killed her."

"You've just made yourself a loose end, man. A loose fucking end."

Henry smirked. "Well, let's hope you kill me properly."

When Roger raised the gun, Henry wondered which of the senses the bullet would sever first. Would he hear it before he felt it? Would it hurt? Maybe, if he was lucky, it would be nothing but numbness, and he'd be cast into oblivion to join the mist silently and painlessly. But the longer he waited, the more he realized it wasn't coming.

Slowly, he opened his eyes. He saw Roger's chin pointing toward the ceiling, his face turning an ugly shade of purple. Henry felt the dead around him. Normally, it would cause pressure on his skull, or an indistinct throb behind his temples. Now, it felt different. Now, they were using him, feeding on him. This world was theirs now.

As Henry watched the toes of Roger's shoes leave the floor and his head stretch toward the ceiling, he didn't feel fear. As he saw the man's neck struggle for air against the strength of a phantom limb wrapped around it, Henry didn't wish he was anywhere else. As far as he was concerned, this was Stacey's moment. Stacey's justice. If she wanted to take Henry too, use his body, and talent, as sacrifice, she was welcome to it. She was welcome to him.

Around him, he watched the room succumb to the power of the supernatural. The lights flickered and the bedsheets shivered. In the room's corner, a stretch of peeling wallpaper vibrated. Henry couldn't see the dead, but he tasted them. The atmosphere felt horrible, thick and heavy in his mouth, and for a moment, Waxwing Creek didn't feel evil at all.

Roger started choking. Henry watched ghostly fingers make their way into the man's mouth, protruding his cheeks, stretching down his throat. Roger fought it, and Henry saw their tips pushing against the canals inside his neck.

And then came its conclusion. Roger's neck severed, and whatever ghost was lodged in its tubes exploded. It spread bits of Roger's blood and flesh across the motel room, as if a spark had ignited. The bulbs blew and the bed shook. Then the whole motel rattled on its foundations.

Henry ducked, covering his head as the pulse pushed from the room's center to its walls. The table's legs left the carpet, the springs in the mattress vibrated, and a framed print, hanging on the wall above the bed, shuddered.

The remains of Roger's corpse met the floor with a slap. Henry sat, staring at the man's blood on his colorful suit and how it would look if someone entered the room. As he looked at the bone peeking through the bottom of the man's blue neck, he didn't care if someone walked in. As he stared at the thick syrup of blood, all he could feel—all he wanted to feel—was enlightened.

Let in as opposed to pushed out.

Saved.

Redeemed.

Like a man reborn.

MAYHIM

2012

BRIGHT LIGHTS BLOOMED in front of Tariq. The crowd erupted, shaking the foundations of the club's basement. He raised his drumsticks with aching arms, staring at the thrum of people who had, for the last thirty minutes, molded their mouths around lyrics he'd written in a place far from their hometown of Hunt. He looked at strangers wearing t-shirts emblazoned with his band's logo. *Mayhim.* A name they'd chosen on a whim three years ago, not thinking it would amount to anything. But it had amounted to something. It was unusual, just two people in a band, but they'd made it work.

He looked at Grayson, his best friend and bandmate. With one hand over the microphone, the other resting on an electric guitar, Tariq could see he was hurting.

But he didn't care. He didn't want to think about Grayson. Not now. All he wanted was the noise of the crowd, a rising tide so strong he hoped it would pull him under.

And then technicians turned off the lights, and the stage

went dark. Tariq and Grayson disappeared, made enigmas for another night.

Tariq pushed himself off the stool and used the bottom of his sleeveless vest to wipe away the sweat pooled under his hairline. He noted the generic soundtrack playing and the drone of the audience talking over each other, looking for friends lost in the crowd.

Tariq pushed past a couple guys working the venue, feeling their hands slapping his back. When he reached the green room, he was relieved to find it empty, a couple beers waiting on a table. He looked at himself in one of the mirrors. Its surface, marred with a long crack and dried stains, showed a face that was tired but elated, still glowing with adrenaline.

In its reflection, he saw Grayson enter in the ripped black jeans and t-shirt he wore every night. Bleach blond hair showed its natural brown at the roots. The tattoos that slithered up his arms and neck looked blurry, and his eyebrow piercing was infected.

"You alright, man?" Tariq said into the reflection. Grayson said nothing, just dropped onto the worn leather couch and opened one of the beers with a satisfying click.

Tariq felt irritation swell. He thought of the last nights, packing up the equipment alone, standing at the merch table solo, spending nights in the van while Grayson was off doing whatever he was doing. This was the last gig of this run; their first run. It should be a time to celebrate.

Grayson collapsed the now empty can and threw it into the corner.

"Dude. What's going on?"

"Nothing," Grayson said, opening the second can, standing to leave.

"Doesn't look like nothing," Tariq said, throwing his chin to the drink.

Grayson hurled himself toward Tariq so quickly he didn't have time to register the shock. Tariq felt his back against the wall, his friend's hand around his neck, shaking the mirror where it hung.

"What did you just say?" Grayson's eyes looked wild and feral. When Tariq felt fingers pressing into his windpipe, he slammed his hands against his friend's chest so hard Grayson stumbled and started coughing against the impact.

"Don't fucking touch me, man. What's wrong with you?" Tariq analyzed him, anticipating an answer, watching Grayson wrap his hands around his body, spent by the outburst. On the other side of the room, someone appeared at the door, blowing the tension away.

"Hey, you two wanna..." The voice trailed off. Tariq didn't need to look to know it was Graham, a bassist from another band on the line-up. "Everything okay?"

"Everything's fine," Grayson said, eyes still locked with Tariq. "I was just leaving."

Tariq watched him go.

"What's up with him?"

"Nothing," Tariq lied. "He'll be alright."

"Alright. Me and the others are gonna head out after we tear down. See what this city's got going for it. You in?"

"Sure, man. I'll catch you up."

IT HAD BEEN three days since Tariq had seen Grayson. Three days of sending messages and calling but hearing nothing back. After the gig, they'd driven back to Hunt together. The journey had been long, out of the city onto quiet and forested roads, spent entirely in silence.

When Tariq dropped him at his apartment and helped him unload his gear, he'd caught his eye, hoping it would be enough to break the ice. Only, it hadn't. Grayson had closed the door without a goodbye, and Tariq hadn't heard from him since.

The sound of his phone vibrating made him jump, bringing him back to an engine that needed service and the comfort of an empty road. He brought his car back in line with the tarmac's markings, seeing his girlfriend's name on his phone in the dark.

"Hey."

"Are you driving?"

"No." Tariq smiled.

"Liar."

"What's up?"

"I just passed Grayson's car."

"What? Where?"

"Parked outside Waxwing."

"You're kidding."

"I'm not."

"Well, did you see him? Was he with anybody?"

"Nope. Just his car."

"And you're sure it was his?"

"I'm sure."

Tariq thought about the motel. Thought back to the first and only time they'd visited. Waxwing Creek had been in their orbit for as long as Tariq could remember. It was part of the package when growing up in Hunt. It had a reputation and presence so pronounced it had become part of the town's folklore. Part of its atmosphere. While everybody had a different story about it, and any poor soul who'd stayed there would have something different to say, the conclusion was universal: You leave Waxwing Creek well alone.

But when you're bored on a Wednesday night with nothing but energy drinks and instant noodles in your belly, a place like Waxwing Creek seems like the best idea you've ever had. So, almost six months ago, they'd done what all their friends had said they'd done but hadn't: they booked a room. Why? So they could say they'd written a song there. So they could see what all the fuss was about.

"Tariq?"

"Yeah, yeah. I'm here."

"What are you gonna do?"

He'd already turned the car around. Before he'd said it out loud, he'd committed the tires to a different direction.

"I'm heading over there. I want to know what's going on."

"Are you sure? Do you want me to come?"

"No, no. If something is happening, it's probably best it's just me. But we're still on for later, right? I'll come over after."

"Yeah, of course... Be careful, babe."

"I was born careful." Tariq laughed. "Waxwing Creek ain't got nothing on me."

* * *

By the time Tariq reached the motel, dusk had turned to dark, and he wondered if Grayson would still be there. When he passed its sign, its dusted parking lot, filled only with his friend's vehicle, he wasn't sure whether to give in to fear or relief.

He passed the motel, pulling off the road and cutting

the engine. If Grayson was hanging around, Tariq didn't want him to know he was there. Not yet. Pulling his hood around his head, he exited and locked the car, taking a moment to look around.

A lot of forest wrapped around Hunt, but here, it felt different. The trees seemed endless, stretching into a threatening eternity of heavy trunks and thick wooden limbs.

Using the motel as a lighthouse, he approached, scared that if he circled too wide, the forest would swallow him. He arrived at the back of the building and made his way to the gap in the curtains of the only room that had a light on.

He saw Grayson knelt on the floor. He was alone, a towel set out in front of him with a plastic cup resting on top. He had his t-shirt rolled up so its sleeves bunched at his shoulders. He could see his friend shaking.

Before he'd registered the box cutter, Grayson had slid the metal across the top of his forearm, deep enough that blood pooled around the line, overspilling and running down Grayson's skin like ink.

Tariq watched as Grayson grit his teeth against the pain, straightening his arm out, elbow to the floor. Through the window, he heard his friend grunt, pressing hard into the wound to encourage the flow, and he watched as Grayson guided the blood, rolling it to the tips of his fingers where it could drop into the plastic cup.

Tariq swore under his breath. He felt a new layer of sweat emerging over the dampness that was already there. He didn't know what was happening, but he didn't like it. He wanted to turn away. To run. He felt like he was invading his best friend's privacy. Watching him vulnerable, lost in one of his most intimate moments. Grayson pushed on the wound, and the blood kept coming, kept funneling its way into the container, and Tariq couldn't help but watch.

Then, Grayson stopped. He sat back, threw his head to the sky, and started crying.

"Why aren't you coming?" Grayson moaned. "I've given you enough. I've given you enough."

Tariq hated it. Hated the distress and the pain. Hated seeing his friend like this. He was about to break in and end it, scoop the boy up in his arms and take him to his family and friends so they could stage an intervention and find help. Real help.

But then Grayson started smiling. He saw relief as Grayson threw his arms out.

"You came," he said. "You came!"

Tariq peered into the room, trying to see who he was talking to.

"And you have to change it," Grayson continued. "You've got to take it away... But I don't *want* it. I don't want any of it."

Tariq furrowed his eyebrows, confused.

"I know, I know," Grayson said. "But I don't want that anymore. You have to stop them hurting me."

Silence.

"No. I came here alone."

Grayson turned his head to meet Tariq, and Tariq's world blew apart. He cursed, pushing himself from the window so hard he fell back, tripping on a log and landing on his ass. He scrambled, feeling leaves, soil, and rotten wood push under his nails as he tried to regain his footing.

As Grayson rounded the back of the motel, Tariq had already started running through the forest to his car, feeling the branches and leaves whipping at his arms and legs, feeling the reflections from the leaves following his every move. He wanted to look behind him, to see how close Grayson was, but knew it would cost him time. Could cost him everything.

If he hadn't tripped, he would have made it. If that log hadn't been there, and he hadn't hit the dirt so hard it knocked the wind out of his lungs, he would have gotten away. He felt a hand on his back, in his hair, and a force that pulled Tariq around to face his friend.

"Who are you?" Grayson screamed, one hand on Tariq's head, the other holding the box cutter to his throat.

"Dude, it's Tee. It's Tariq!"

"Tariq? What the fuck are you doing here, man? Have you been following me?"

"No, no, no."

"Well, what are you doing?"

"I was worried about you. You haven't been yourself. I could see you were hurting after the show. And...and I don't know what drugs you're on, man."

"It isn't drugs."

"So what it is? What were you doing back there?"

Grayson shook his head. From where Tariq was lying, his eyes looked like two pools—filled with shadows.

"You really want to see it?"

Tariq didn't know how to answer. Part of him wanted truth. The other part didn't want to return to that motel, to that room, with all that blood. But he was strewn on the forest's ground with a friend who needed him and a knife still warm from the heat of his throat. So he nodded and, realizing Grayson may not be able to see him, committed to a "yes" out loud.

Grayson put his hand out. When he grabbed it, it felt like they were friends again, teenagers glued to the bedroom floor, attempting to stitch chords and melodies together in a way that transcended simplicity.

Together, they made their way back to the motel, encountering no one on the way, to a room that smelled stale and metallic, like the window had been closed for years. Tariq could see the towel stained with drops of blood that had missed the cup. The walls were old, the carpet tired. Behind him, he heard Grayson close the door and lock it.

"Gray—" Tariq began.

"What did you see?" Grayson's voice was quiet, cutting him off.

"Dude."

"What did you see?"

"You cut yourself," Tariq said.

"Then what?"

"And then drained the blood into that cup."

"After that," he said, rotating a lazy wrist.

"You started speaking to someone. Talking about something."

Grayson raised his head to meet Tariq's gaze and broke apart. "I've fucked up, man. I've really fucked up."

"Gray," Tariq said, "what have you been taking? If I know what it is, I'll know how I can help."

"I told you, it's not drugs," Grayson yelled. "Stop saying it's fucking drugs! We promised each other we wouldn't do that."

"Alright, alright. But you've gotta give me something. I'm struggling here, man."

"You remember the last time we were here?"

"I remember."

"Well, I came back. The night after, I came back."

"What? Why?"

"Because I felt something. Heard something. The first time. I just didn't tell you."

The rapid beating of Tariq's heart thrummed in his ears. He thought back to that night. Questioned whether he'd felt something. Asked himself whether he'd heard something, but he kept coming up blank. "What did you feel, Gray?"

"A promise," he whispered. "She told me she could make us huge."

"Who did?"

Grayson continued, ignoring him. "She told me she could make them love us. She promised me people would *want* us. And it worked. The video went viral. We got the radio play. The momentum. It all started that next morning. You remember, right? How it all just came together so suddenly? Then we booked the tour and the tickets sold out. Sure, they were small venues, in small towns, but it was happening for us."

"I remember."

"But that first night we played, I noticed something. Their claps. Their shouts. When they *sang* with us." Tariq noticed Grayson growing angry, forcing the words through gritted teeth. "It hurt so much, man." He started crying again. "I got through it. I pushed on. But the second show was worse. So I sang louder, but that only encouraged them. Every sound those people made felt like cuts. By the last night, I wanted it to kill me. I finished that set wanting to die."

To Tariq, it almost made sense. Almost. He'd seen the change. Their music picked up out of nowhere. He thought it was algorithms, luck, fate. But he'd also seen the warning signs. He'd seen Grayson replace his love for music with impatience for fame. He'd heard the jokes he'd make to friends, saying what he'd do in exchange for a record deal.

"So why did you come back? Why are you cutting yourself?"

"To speak with her," he said, blade still in hand. "She told me if I ever wanted to speak with her again, I had to bleed for it."

"And that's what you've been doing? Cutting yourself?"

"That's what I've been doing. So I can tell her I don't want it anymore. So she can take it all away. But I didn't get to that. Because *you* were watching."

"Dude."

"So I've gotta do it again." He moaned. "I've gotta give her more."

"No way," Tariq said. "We are getting you to a hospital. You've lost a lot of blood. That cut needs stitches."

Tariq watched him. Saw the cogs in his friend's brain turning themselves over, working it all out. Then he saw the cogs stop, and an idea settle into place.

"You can do it."

"What?"

"You can give her some. You can call her for me."

"Oh no, no, no, no, no." Tariq panicked. "We're leaving now, Grayson. My car is outside. We've just got to—"

"No! After everything I've given for us. After everything I've given for you. You *owe* me this."

"Dude, listen to yourself. You sound crazy. We're going to get you out of here. We're going to get you help. Tonight."

Before Tariq could say anything else, Grayson rushed at him. Tariq grabbed Grayson's arm, holding it, and the blade, away from him, hoping his friend's strength had been sapped from the loss of blood. He forced the palm of his other hand under Grayson's chin, pushing as hard as he could.

When he felt Grayson twist his wrist, Tariq let out a yell, feeling a sharp pain shoot up his fingers to his elbow. That's all it took. A moment of pain, a release of pressure, and Tariq went from keeping the blade away to watching it sink into his chest. He stumbled, feeling the top of the bedside table hit the bottom of his back. His fingers reached for the wound, instinctively trying to hold its two sides together.

He drew his fingers back, seeing them soaked with blood. He looked at Grayson, his best friend, his bandmate, box cutter in hand, yellow handle stained red. He'd expected the blood would signal Grayson to stop, that it would cause enough of a shock to make Grayson reexamine what he was doing. But all he saw in his friend's eyes was possibility. Hunger. An opportunity, Tariq guessed, to bring his woman back.

"It's not enough," Grayson whispered.

He moved for Tariq again, sinking the blade into his shoulder. Tariq didn't scream, but looked at Grayson with eyes spread wide. When the knife came down again, into his cheek, hitting his teeth, he knew Grayson wasn't going to stop. When it sliced his neck, Tariq knew he was going to die.

As Grayson plunged the blade into his flesh again and again, and the life started to seep out of Tariq's body, he saw something in the room change.

He saw the walls of Waxwing Creek turn a darker shade, as though wet. From their tops, at the seam where they met the ceiling, they started bleeding blood so vibrant, Tariq wondered whether it was real or a hallucination from the pain.

As his vision started to fade to black, to purple, to the color of his death, he saw those walls move. He saw the woman Grayson had been talking about take form, the walls shifting around her figure. And then he heard Grayson laugh as something stepped out of the red mass and gave physical form to liquid.

THE HUNT

2019

WHEN PHOEBE OPENED the door to room two, she'd been expecting dirt and tangled cobwebs. Instead, a sparse yet serviceable room greeted her: A bed in the middle, a bedside table with a lamp, and an uncomfortable wooden chair in the corner. The gap between the curtains revealed the forest behind Waxwing Creek, all inky darkness, broken apart by reflections on wet leaves that looked like eyes. It unsettled her, so she pulled the curtains closed.

"Two nights," she said with a sigh, tossing her suitcase onto the bed. "Two nights and you're out."

Phoebe hated living out of a suitcase, so she made a point of emptying it every time she traveled. She placed her clothes on top of the dresser, scared to reveal what a place like this could be hiding inside its drawers. She put her spare shoes together by the door and her toiletries in the bathroom, arranging them on the small surface between the sink and the wall.

Finally, she took her laptop out of her handbag, brushed its surface down, rested it on the dresser beside her clothes, and plugged it into one of the room's outlets.

As she waited for it to connect to the Wi-Fi, she moved into the bathroom, running the warm water so she could remove her contact lenses and wash the day from her face. When she returned to her laptop, its search had finished, highlighting a large exclamation mark to let her know the connection had failed. She'd expected this to happen in a place like Waxwing Creek but, not wanting to leave her room and ask about internet in the office, decided to tether her phone.

After a while she connected, moved to the bed, and clicked the photo of her sister, Lena.

"Hey, Phoebs. Wait a minute, will you?"

"What are you doing?"

"Just wait a minute."

Phoebe waited, rearranging herself to sit cross-legged on the duvet. She checked her hair in the camera, noticing for the first time the hard texture of the bed's headboard behind her, and an unassuming print of an ocean above it.

"Alright," her sister said. "I'm listening."

"What were you doing?"

"Just replying to Alex. How's Hunt?"

"Honestly? Kind of tragic."

"You want to know what else is tragic?"

"What?"

"That wallpaper."

"Lena, you would not be able to cope here. Like, at all."

"I still can't believe that other motel fucked up your booking."

"Don't. I mean, of course there's an elk hunt this week-end. Place is overrun with gun-toting assholes."

"Did you get a refund for that?"

"For the motel? Yeah, yeah."

"Then stop being so dramatic. It's two nights, and need

I remind you that it was *your* choice to go there? You could have done what you need to do somewhere a little less... remote. It's only for school."

"It's for my *thesis*," Phoebe said. "Not enough people understand how important soil is for... You know what, forget it."

"Well, go on then..." Lena sighed. "Give us a tour."

"Alright," Phoebe said, groaning as she pushed herself off the bed. She lifted her laptop, swiveling it so the camera could take in the entirety of the room. "Here we have a window that looks out to Hunt's creepy-looking forest, this dresser, and a wooden chair that no one would want to sit on. And here..." she continued, swinging her body so the camera looked over her shoulder to the room's other side, "is the bed, with fuck knows what stains on it and bugs *in* it, a door that catches on the frame, and that tiny, little excuse for a room there is the bathroom."

"You know, for a motel that's had so much wild shit happen to it, it's kind of a letdown."

"Wild shit?"

"Didn't you google the place before you got there?"

"Lena, it was my only option. I didn't exactly have time to... Actually, I don't wanna know. Keep it to yourself." Phoebe groaned, moving to the foot of the bed, where she put the laptop on the dresser. In the camera, she could see the expanse of the wall behind her. She put her head in her hands and started talking to the floor. "How's Mom?"

"She's good," Lena said.

"She spoken to the doctor about those headaches yet?"

"She's got an appointment tomorrow evening. Hey, where did you go?"

"I'm here," Phoebe said, looking up.

"I can't see you. It's like, all zoomed in or something."

Phoebe pushed herself up, moving closer to her laptop.

"There you are! What was that?"

"My laptop's got this face-tracking thing on the camera," Phoebe said, readjusting the screen.

"Face-tracking thing?"

"Yeah. It's one of those that zooms in to whoever's speaking. Follows you around the room so you're always in shot. Clearly, it thinks that picture above the bed looks like a face. Better now?"

"Yeah, I can see you. Anyway, I should get some sleep, and so should you. I bet you're tired after all that traveling."

"Yeah. Tomorrow's pretty—"

"Ugh, Phoebe, it's doing it again."

"I see it," Phoebe said. "Why is it *doing* that?"

"I dunno," Lena said. "But it seems to like that picture."

"Weird," Phoebe said, eyebrows creased, fingers scrambling across the laptop's trackpad.

"Maybe it isn't a picture of an ocean. Maybe it's a face. A *dead* face."

"Oh, shut up, Lena."

"Maybe it's one of the Dakotas."

"Who are the Dakotas?"

"You know, it really wouldn't hurt to look up where you're staying."

"Lena, I'm the one who has to sleep here tonight, so can you *please* shut the fuck up."

"Alright, alright. I'll catch you tomorrow. I'll call you after Mom's appointment."

"Alright. Love you."

"Love you."

Phoebe shut the laptop, killing the conversation and the voice that brought her so much comfort. She didn't know if it was the tiredness from the trip or what her sister had said, but she felt everything Lena had left unsaid about Waxwing Creek weighing on her.

So, she began an internal struggle: ignore her sister, or look up the motel's legacy. In the time it took her to get ready for bed, she managed to keep the doubts at bay. By the time she started to hear people in the rooms beside her shouting and swearing and car engines growling outside, the light from her phone shone on her face, and her fingers started scrolling.

She knew she shouldn't have. If anything was going to keep her awake, it was the story of a motel built on top of a dead family. More than that, there were the reviews. Dirty bedrooms. Bad customer service. And yes, bugs crawling in the beds. News reports spanning years talked of murder and malicious intent. From what she'd read, the motel had changed hands only a month ago. Why its new owner had chosen to keep its name was a mystery to her. It was like the motel's legacy was a drug, a dangerous pill, and no number of fresh starts would ever get it clean.

Eventually, sleep came. Broken and unsettled, but enough to push her through to the morning, when the sun streamed through the curtains and the sound of shots from an elk hunt filled the air.

***

Fog hung so heavy over Hunt's forest, it looked like someone had draped it over the trees. The air was chilly, blistered with the sounds of gunshots that had rung out all morning. Phoebe had asked at the office where the hunt was taking place, hoping to complete her work as far from the commotion as possible. Dressed in her yellow rain jacket, she'd run her fingers through the soil, collected the samples from the locations she'd plotted beforehand, and put them in small plastic containers labeled with her name, date, and coordinates. When she returned to Waxwing Creek, she was tired, hungry, and more than ready to go home.

Outside, the day's light had turned dark, and the hunt around Hunt had quieted when Phoebe's phone ignited with her sister's name.

"Hey."

"Hey," Lena replied.

"Let me call you back on my laptop."

"Why?"

"I just prefer it. Two minutes."

Phoebe tethered her phone in the same way she had the night before, placing her laptop on the dresser so she could call her sister back.

"Hey."

"Hey," Phoebe said. "How's Mom?"

"Ah, she's okay. Same old doctor. Brand new pills. We'll see how it goes. How'd work go today?"

"Fine. I got what I needed, but thanks to that damn elk hunt, I didn't have as much freedom as I thought I would."

"You know, for someone pursuing a career in research, you're really bad at it." The truth of it forced a laugh out of Phoebe, and she saw her sister smile in response. "Oh my God, Phoebs. Can you sort your camera out? Turn that tracking thing off or move or something. I'm going to call you back on your phone."

"It's going for that picture again."

"Call me back on your phone."

"No, wait. I hate talking on that thing."

"Well, take that picture down, at least."

"Alright," Phoebe said, climbing onto the bed. She reached up, stretching out her hand to remove the print from its place. "Fuck!" The shout escaped Phoebe with force, and she pulled her hand to her chest as if it had been burned.

"What?"

"I–I dunno," Phoebe stammered, heart pounding. "Something grabbed me."

"What are you talking about?"

"Something fucking grabbed me, Lena."

Phoebe was sweating. Panicking. The skin on her arms and neck ignited with goosebumps. Her head throbbed from the shot of adrenaline.

"What do you mean, something grabbed you?" She could hear the disbelief in her sister's voice.

Her mind went to what she'd read the night before: stories of the Dakotas, tales of a family found dead, accounts of endless horrors witnessed by the same walls surrounding her now. While she didn't know if those stories were true, she knew hers was. She'd felt cold skin on her hand. She'd sensed the pressure of flesh split into fingers pressing into her veins.

"I felt something. A– A... I don't know. It wrapped itself around my hand. It was cold. The whole room is cold."

"You been drinking, girl?"

"Jesus, Lena! For once, just listen to what I'm saying. I'm scared."

"Oh my God." The tone of Lena's voice sounded so shocked it slid through the small holes of the laptop's speakers.

"What?" Phoebe whispered, eyes snapping to the screen. "*What?*"

"Do you see what I'm seeing?"

"Oh my God," Phoebe echoed. She saw it. Saw it as clearly as her sister did. The laptop's camera was following something, tracking something, zooming in and then pulling itself out so it could fit both Phoebe and whatever it was on the screen. It started at the ocean print, moving across the room's wallpaper until it stopped.

"Okay, I am seriously freaking the fuck *out*," Phoebe shouted at the camera, throwing her hands above her head. "I'm checking out. I'm coming home. No way am I staying here tonight."

Lena sounded her agreement.

Of all the things that could have, or should have, been terrifying, Lena's approval scared her most. Her sister was the one who denied these things. Now she was agreeing. She wasn't stopping Phoebe from leaving.

"And you're staying on that laptop until I'm packed."

She rushed into the bathroom, grabbing her toothbrush, hairbrush, creams and ointments in one hand, opening her wash bag with the other.

"Phoebe?" Her sister's voice sounded distant, as though struggling to find its way from the dresser.

"Yeah, I'm fine."

"No, you're going to want to see this."

"See what?"

"The picture."

"Ugh, Lena. Stop! I don't want to know."

"It's moving. The frame is moving."

Nausea slammed into Phoebe's gut. Part of her wanted to close the bathroom door, lean over the toilet, and let the stress out. Let it all out. The other part of her wanted to take it out on her sister. To shout and scream and tell her to get a grip. If this was her messing around, the joke had been taken too far.

She closed her eyes and bit her bottom lip, hoping the pain would bring some clarity.

"Lena, I swear to God, if I come around that corner and that frame isn't moving, I'm going to—"

But it was. The bottom of the picture's frame lifted from the wall and dropped, slowly then with speed, tapping hard against the wallpaper's textured surface.

"*Fuck*," Phoebe moaned. "What is going on?"

The tapping stopped. The frame rested firm and quiet against the wall's hard surface. Phoebe had been about to launch into her sister about the ridiculousness of what she was saying. But she couldn't get away from the timing of the tapping. How its stopping had felt like an answer.

"Phoebs? You still there?"

"I'm here," she whispered.

"Alright," Lena said. Phoebe could tell her sister was trying to instill her own calm. She, too, was fighting the fear. "Pack your bags and get in the car. I'm not going anywhere."

She listened, moving from the bathroom. She forced her eyes from the picture, throwing her suitcase onto the bed. She picked up her clothes from the dresser, her glasses from the bedside table, unplugged the laptop's charger, and fed the case like it was an open mouth.

"You're doing great. Do you have everything?"

"I think so," Phoebe said. "And even if I don't, it doesn't matter. There's no way I'm looking under the bed."

"How are you going to take the laptop? Will the connection cut out?"

"It shouldn't. It's tethered to my phone. You're staying with me until I'm home."

"Of course."

"Okay." Phoebe sighed, leaning over the case to pull its zip closed. "I'm leaving now." She picked it up, enjoying the sensation of it pulling at her wrist. It was something real in all this madness. She stuffed her feet into her shoes and picked up her laptop. Seeing her sister's face, as pixelated and small as it was, filled her with so much comfort she thought she might cry.

Without looking back, Phoebe put her hand on the door's handle and turned. She expected to see lights and the road, the forest and her car, but all that met her was the mass of something on the other side, pushing her back into the room.

A clambering of feet entered the space she'd slept in for two days. Not supernatural. Human. Real feet that belonged to a real person that smelt of sweat and unwashed clothes. She stumbled, falling onto her back, dropping her laptop. She tried to scream as a warm, clammy hand pressed hard against her mouth.

A YEAR HAD PASSED. Three hundred and sixty-five days filled with suffering and aches so severe, Lena had started drinking to make them go away. Fifty-two weeks of hoping she'd be able to hear her sister's voice again.

Hunt flew past her in a blur of dark colors. The roads here seemed directionless, flanked by trees that drooped with rain. A forest like that was meant to look pretty, beautiful even. Only, it was oppressive. As she passed the same buildings and homes she knew her sister had a year before, Lena tightened her grip on the steering wheel, shaking when her destination finally appeared before her.

Waxwing Creek.

For Lena, the last year had been a lifetime. For Waxwing Creek, it was another year of business. Another year of putting a roof over the heads of drifters, delinquents, and people like her sister who made the mistake of getting caught up in its mess.

The motel stood before her like a parasite, and she loathed it. She wanted to tear the walls from its foundation with her teeth and rip up its dirtied carpets until her fingers bled. She wanted to fill it with the same venom that filled her and burn it to the ground.

A year ago, it would have taken a lot of courage for Lena to do what she readied herself to do now. It would have taken her everything to invite chaos into her life. But she knew she needed to do it, not just for herself, but for Phoebe. She'd poured the last year of her life into this theory and was finally ready to put it to bed. So, when she leaned over to grab the gun out of the glove compartment and hid it in her jacket pocket, she felt empowered, like a woman who could kill.

Lena got out of the car, making her way to the office at the end of the motel's long line of doors.

"Evening," said the woman behind the desk, glancing over the glasses positioned on the end of her nose. "Looking for a room?"

"I booked," Lena said. It was a different woman from the one who'd owned the motel when Phoebe went missing, but that didn't mean she didn't know something. Maybe bringing out the gun would encourage her to spill it. Maybe it would just make Lena feel better.

"Name?"

"Lena," she said. "Lena Manners." To Lena, it was the first test, to see if the woman recognized the name.

"Alright, Lena Manners," she said sarcastically. "You're in room three."

"That's not right," Lena said.

"Excuse me?"

"Room two. I have to be in room two."

"Not possible. Room two is booked tonight. It's the weekend of the hunt. I can't ..."

Lena panicked, feeling her power, her theory, slipping away. "I'll pay! Name your price, and I'll pay it." She felt tears gather in the corners of her eyes and a lump forming in her throat. She searched for the firmness of the pistol in her pocket, expecting the woman to turn her away, deny her, but she was surprised to see the stranger's face soften.

"Alright. You're lucky our other guests haven't arrived yet. Room two it is."

Lena breathed a sigh of relief. The woman pushed away from the desk to the back of the office, returning with a keyring printed with the room's number.

Lena took it and, without saying good evening or thank you, left.

She stepped outside, grateful for the cool air on her face. The door to room two stood stoic, and she wondered if its silver number was as rusted when Phoebe had opened it a year ago. She pushed the thought away, took one last look at the forest with leaves that looked like eyes, and unlocked it.

She remembered the tour Phoebe had given her, welling up at how much she missed the sarcasm in her voice. The wallpaper she'd hated was still there, and the bathroom was as small as she remembered it. And there it was. The picture of the ocean, still unassuming, still tired, that they'd both seen lifted by phantom fingers.

She transferred the key between anxious hands, feeling her sister there so completely she could have reached out and embraced her. She almost did. If it hadn't been for her theory, the weapon in her pocket, Waxwing Creek may have broken her. But she wouldn't let that happen.

Not today.

As she made her way to the window to close the curtains, she thought about the events that had led her there, going over everything in case she'd missed something.

When she'd found reports of the first missing person, appeals from the parents and family, she'd been fueled not by astonishment but sadness. When she found the second and third, a disturbing pattern of disappearances she couldn't believe authorities had missed, the sadness had hardened to anger. There had been years between the first and second, but she found they all had one thing in common: they'd been women visiting Hunt on the weekend of an elk hunt, and they'd been staying at Waxwing Creek Motel.

She took her discovery to the police, calling for updates every day, turning up at the station drunk and depressed demanding answers. They'd removed her by force, and she presumed the case had been lost. So, Lena decided to wait an endless year until the elk hunt came around. To take matters into her own hands by putting herself in the place of the victim.

Her fingers wrapped themselves around the pistol's grip. The print of the ocean stared at her, its crashing whites and rolling blues out of place in the bland room. But she was glad to see it. Even after a change of hands and an awful year, the print, like her, had survived.

She made her way toward it. She eased herself onto the bed, preparing for it to shake. When it didn't, she stretched out her hand. Still, it didn't move. With one knee on the bed, one foot on the floor, she lifted it from the screw it was resting on, almost hoping it would bite.

In the picture she saw something odd: a perfect circle, small and discreet, cut away from the print's ink. Then she saw what was in the wall behind it. She saw herself reflected in the camera's lens, and the parts came together so effortlessly Lena swore she heard them all slot together in her mind.

She saw how the camera was positioned, with a clear view of the bed and the bathroom. She imagined its lens zooming in and out to better focus on whoever it was watching. Her mind went to the women who'd gone missing over the years. Which of those ghosts had tried to warn her sister a year ago? Which of those women had pushed through the evil of Waxwing Creek to try to save her life?

Then she thought of who was on the other side, watching, waiting. What creep would set something up like this and wait with such patience? She didn't have to imagine long because she heard movement. Behind her, the door to her motel room opened. She heard it close and lock, and she smiled.

Lena put the picture back on its screw and turned to face it, pistol ready in hand.

GLORIA

2020

Robert Callahan took another sip of coffee, watching as the police pulled a body out of room two of Waxwing Creek. It wasn't the first time he'd seen a corpse dragged out of that motel, but he hoped, as he had for years, that it would be his last.

He didn't know anything about the victim. Not yet. The details would emerge in the paper, on the radio, and get tossed around the town of Hunt with no regard for who would hear them. They'd mention the victim's name, age, who they'd left behind. If the victim was lucky, they'd get a quote or two from a loving family member. But Robert wasn't interested in that. All he wanted was the truth.

Around him, lights soaked the trees in neon blue. He pulled his collar against the cold and a growing uncertainty that the forest's leaves were watching. He saw Jeremiah Landen emerge from the room with a gun strapped to his belt and stress highlighted on his face. His rise in Hunt's police department had been slow but steady. He'd divorced his wife but not his job, and he had a career that was mostly unmarred by controversy. In short, this wasn't the first time he'd responded to something at Waxwing Creek.

As he talked to a fellow officer and then the motel's owner, Robert eyed him, staring hard in the hopes the man would turn and catch his eye.

Finally, he did. He nodded, and without a word, the meeting was set. When Jeremiah ended his shift, helped with the clean-up, the paperwork, whatever it was that needed to be done when someone died, he'd head to a bar called Roseland in the middle of Hunt where Robert would buy him a drink and offer money in exchange for information on what had really happened.

ROBERT WATCHED Jeremiah empty the bottle, the red lights of Roseland highlighting the heavy bags under his eyes.

"You want another?"

Jeremiah waved the question away, stifling a burp. He looked different without his uniform, but Robert was glad for it. Establishments like Roseland didn't take kindly to cops.

"So," Robert said, "tell me."

"Pretty fucking brutal." Jeremiah sighed.

"Victim?"

"Male. Forty-something. Not from around here."

"Cause of death?"

"One bullet in the leg, three in the face, two in the balls. I'll let your imagination decide which killed him."

"And the killer. You get him?"

"Her," Jeremiah said. "She was there, sitting on the bed with blood on her hands holding a cup of cold water. She didn't even seem upset. In fact, I'd go as far as to say she was happy about the whole thing. Gave herself up soon as we arrived."

"What was her name?"

"I can't tell you that."

"Well, did she have a motive?"

"Her sister went missing last year—during the hunt—while she was staying at Waxwing Creek."

Robert grunted.

"Said the police did such a shit job of finding out what happened, she decided to take matters into her own hands. She believes the man she killed did it. So, I guess you could say justice has been served. Just not by us."

"And what do you think?"

"Honestly?" Jeremiah paused. He stopped peeling the label on his bottle and settled his eyes on Robert. "I think it's time you moved on, Robert. Put all this behind you. No more meetings. No more questions. No more trying to put pieces together from the séance that aren't there."

Robert stared at him in disbelief. "But..."

"But nothing," Jeremiah said. "I know what happened to your wife was barbaric. I know you want answers. But it's been more than 30 years, man. If I had answers, I would give them to you, but this is a straight-up revenge shooting. No supernatural entities. No ghosts. No spines hanging out of any mouths."

"I don't believe you."

"Well, you should. It happened. It is what it is."

"I spoke to *everyone* who was at Waxwing Creek that night. Everyone except Cliff and Annabelle. They all said what happened was—"

"Unexplainable. I know, I know." Jeremiah sighed, holding a hand up. "You've told me a thousand times. But it ain't worth nothing without any proof."

"What about Roger then? Roger Jackson."

"What about him?"

"When they found him—when *you* found him—you told me there was no way someone could have severed his neck like that. The way the bones were snapped. You said that yourself."

"Stop." Jeremiah groaned.

"I've spoken with people who've stayed there. People who have seen things. Heard things. *Experienced* things."

"Stop, Robert. Listen to yourself. Life is passing you by. You look so tired."

"So?"

"So, snap out of it! Break the habit. Move on. I'm not telling you as a police officer. I'm telling you as a friend."

"You seeing anyone at the moment?"

"I might be," Jeremiah said.

"You're telling me you wouldn't do the same for them? You're telling me—if something took them away from you— you wouldn't do everything in your power to find out what happened?"

"No, I wouldn't," Jeremiah bit back.

"Why not?"

"Because sometimes you've got to accept reality. Sure, Waxwing Creek's an odd place. Always has been. But do I believe it's harboring a supernatural entity? Do I believe there's a presence in there pulling spines out of people's mouths? No. What I do believe is people get desperate, and cheap places like Waxwing Creek will always be there to catch them. I've been getting calls about that place for years. At the end of the day, you can believe what you want to believe, Rob. But even if there *is* something sinister at work, there's nothing you can do about it, and there's sure as hell nothing you can do to bring your dead wife back."

Robert hadn't expected the words to hurt. He hadn't imagined any of his conversation with Jeremiah to sting as much as it did. As soon as he'd told Robert that there was nothing he could do to bring his wife back, he'd left the bar, got in the car, and headed back to the place he called home. Maybe it was the fact Jeremiah was telling him to give up that cut so close to the bone. Perhaps, deep down, it was because he knew Jeremiah was right. Either way, he'd spent the night tossing and turning, waking only when the sun hit his face through curtains he'd left open.

As he put bread in the toaster, he thought about the moment he found out his wife, Gloria, had died. He'd been in the same bed he'd slept in last night when the phone had erupted in sharp shrills, and he'd woken up sweating. He hadn't heard her leave. Hadn't felt the pressure of their bed shift or heard her slip on the dress she died in. All he woke up to was an indentation in a mattress that needed replacing and a stranger asking if he could come down to the station.

As soon as he heard that voice, he knew what was coming. They didn't have to tell him where she'd been.

For as long as he could remember, Dakota House had been a presence in Hunt. An urban myth with a haunting past, but one that was minding its own business. When Cliff and Annabelle arrived and knocked it down, replacing it with a motel on a road leading out of his small town, something changed. The atmosphere of the place where he'd lived and fallen in love no longer felt like home.

All the séance did was spread that feeling wider and light an ominous fire under Hunt's belly. He remembered the weeks leading up to it. The hushed whispers and hissed insults, petitions, and attempted legalities the people of Hunt tried to put in its way. Long before one of their old neighbors, Amanda McCarthy, developed a crippling fear of germs that would see her never leave her house, she'd visited Cliff and Annabelle herself, pleading with them to stop.

The drama would usually be something Gloria would indulge in. She should have loved the conversational investigation. But when it came to Waxwing Creek, she brushed it off. When Robert had pressed, she'd shown no interest. One evening, she'd even told him to stop talking about it.

If only he'd seen the signs. If only he'd listened to his intuition and put the pieces together.

Gloria had been eleven years old when she'd seen her brother drown. Eleven years old when a stranger had made a decision to pull her out of the same current that smothered her brother to death.

She'd never gotten over it. Never set foot in the ocean again. Maybe she hoped the séance would allow her to speak with him. Maybe she just wanted to see what it would be like to contact the dead.

The toaster popped, bringing Robert back to the cluttered kitchen and a countertop that still held all of Gloria's favorite mugs. He applied butter to the toast and turned toward the table. He couldn't remember the last time he'd seen its dull wooden surface. For years, it had been covered with papers, photographs, and clippings; nuances and echoes of Waxwing Creek collected over the years. Everything that had ever been said about the motel was amassed on its surface, and Robert was confident he had committed most of it to memory.

Included within its mess were the original scraps that spoke of his wife's death. Scraps that didn't mention the way she died or the way her spine had been hanging out of her mouth. No. These were journalists who put it down to murder, and a speculative one at that. Motel owners? Another guest? Someone in Hunt so passionate about halting the séance they'd taken matters into their own hands?

Not once did someone suggest there could be something more sinister at work.

So Robert decided he'd put the pieces together himself. He'd spoken to everyone who had a connection to the séance, and he came to the conclusion that something unfathomable had happened that night at Waxwing Creek. It was more than simple murder.

He sighed, checking his watch. 9:17am. He shuffled his slippers from the kitchen to the front door, opening it to see the local newspaper on the doorstep. He bent down, feeling the weight of old age between the bones of his spine, then stood and opened it. There it was, on the fifth page. Another story to cut out and add to the papers already gathered on the table. A story that should have made the cover but was instead demoted to page five. Perhaps it was that alone that boiled his venom. When had the victims of Waxwing Creek become so trivial? When had murder at the hands of the same motel that had killed his wife been less important than the front page?

He'd thought of doing something before. For years, he'd fantasized about tearing the place down. He'd longed to see the place shut down and for its orifices to be filled with dust and rot. In that moment, with the paper open in front of him and a slice of buttered toast cooling in the kitchen, Robert didn't want any of those things.

That morning, all he wanted was for Waxwing Creek to burn.

BOOKING a room at the motel had been easier than he thought it would be. It was as easy as booking a room at any motel. He didn't know why he'd expected it to be harder or why he'd been sweating when its owner, Clara Alvarez, had answered the phone.

She sounded polite enough. He knew all about her, of course: Purchased the motel with her sister after their father had put a shotgun in his mouth and pulled the trigger. Left a cramped life behind in Chicago for the open roads of Hunt.

But that didn't matter. Robert wasn't here to reminisce about its owner. He wasn't here to put her out of business. As far as he was concerned, he was here to save her life.

He got up from where he sat perched on the bed, moving toward the small suitcase standing by the room's entrance. The room looked as he imagined it would. No number of new owners or fresh starts would revitalize Waxwing Creek. He eased himself down to one knee, using the case to steady his balance while he opened it.

He removed the two-gallon plastic gas canister, aware that in his hands he held the future of this place. With just a few movements and the strike of a match, he could heal all the hurt this wretched motel had caused. When he was ready, he could set this place on fire.

He was just about to unscrew the top and set its memories alight when the door to the bathroom slammed shut behind him. He turned toward it, listening for the silence to fill itself with an answer.

He'd expected to run into whatever haunted Waxwing Creek, but not so soon.

"Hello?" He made sure he shouted it, as much for

himself as for whatever was listening. When nothing responded, he put the canister down and moved toward the bathroom door. He opened it quickly, unafraid, and, on finding the bathroom as empty as it was when he arrived, cursed at his own stupidity.

"You'll have to try harder than that."

When he turned back to the canister and saw his wife Gloria sitting on the bed in the same dress she'd died in, tension clutched his chest.

He closed his eyes, telling himself she was dead, and forced himself to steady his breathing. As he did, he replayed the details of her demise. He thought of the dress she was wearing and the voice of the police officer telling him to come down to the station. Saw visions of a corpse with a spine hanging out of its mouth.

There was no way she could be here.

There was no way she could be alive.

When he reopened his eyes, she was still there, sitting on the bed, smiling.

"Robert," she whispered. "It's okay."

"You're not real."

"I'm not going to hurt you."

"You're not real!" he yelled, leveling a shaking finger at her. "You're not fucking real."

"But I am... Come, darling. Hold me."

He didn't know if it was the way she said "darling" or the look in her eyes when she held out her arms, but something in Robert broke. The part inside him that wanted to believe she was there escaped from where he'd locked it away, breaking free of the dust he'd layered on top of it, unlocking the tears from his eyes and his feet from the floor.

For so long, all he'd dreamed about was her touch. For so long, all he'd dreamed about was seeing her again and staring into those eyes. Now she was so close he could taste it.

As soon as she placed her hands on his, he knew he'd made a mistake. As soon as he felt the presence, like cold, wet leaves on his skin, he knew he'd never be able to finish what he'd set out to do.

"Look at me," Gloria cooed.

With a cold finger, she tilted Robert's head toward her, and instead of meeting the blue eyes he'd fallen in love with, he saw black eyes bordered with tiny teeth, sitting above bones that emerged from an open mouth.

He screamed. Tried to pull away from the grip the thing had on him, cursing himself for falling for it so easily, but it was futile. It wasn't just her hands on him now, but hundreds of them, pressing their fingers, palms, and nails into his body, pulling him back onto the bed.

"You have to understand it can't change," Gloria's voice said as his back hit the mattress, and she moved her legs to straddle him. He tried to yell for help but found only a cold pressure filling his mouth. "Nobody will ever change it. Waxwing Creek must remain the same."

From the edge of his vision, he saw the bright red of the gas canister scraping itself across the room's brittle carpet. Gloria—or what was left of Gloria—disappeared from where she was towering over him and returned with it in her hands.

"No." Robert tried to speak around whatever was in his mouth. Tried to force away the fear lodged in his throat so someone would hear him. "Please," he pleaded. "Don't do this."

But it was too late. The cold on his tongue, his gums, his lips was replaced with something solid, something plastic, and a taste unlike anything he'd experienced started filling his mouth. He tried to spit it out, but there was too much. The fumes of the gasoline tore through his sinuses.

As those fumes were replaced with the realization that he was dying, Robert didn't think of Gloria.

Instead, he thought about Jeremiah. How the police officer would react to finding the body of someone he'd called a friend, and hoped, with everything left in his being, that the man wouldn't be stupid enough to put it down to suicide.

AN ATTEMPT AT ANSWERS

2023

Marcia Martins received the call a week ago, almost to the minute, and hoped the turn in weather wasn't setting a precedent for what was to come. Of all the opportunities she'd been offered in the past, what she was going to attempt today would be her greatest.

As she turned off the main road into Waxwing Creek's parking lot, she saw its dead neon sign and rooms lined up like refrigerators at a morgue. Her stomach dropped. She hadn't expected it to. On the contrary, she'd been excited. Elated. Expectant. Seeing it standing like that, so bleak and barren, she started to question what she'd gotten herself into.

Elena Charr stood where cars should be parked, arms crossed, waiting. She looked skinny to the point of illness, dressed in frayed jeans and a thick jumper, smoking a cigarette so fervently it looked like she was using it to keep warm.

"Marcia," Elena said with a heavy sigh as she stepped out of the vehicle. Marcia could hear the years of nicotine in her voice. The damage it had left there. "You look different from the pictures. Taller. It's so good of you to come. How was the drive?"

"Uneventful," Marcia quipped, slamming the door behind her. "So, this is it? The famous Waxwing Creek."

"This is it," Elena said, turning to face it, blowing a mouthful of smoke out to the side. "Needs a bit of work. A lot of TLC. But I'm hoping today marks a turning point for it. A new beginning."

"Well," Marcia said, "we will try our best."

She made her way to the back of the car, opening the trunk and pulling out the small suitcase she brought to every job. She closed it and, taking one last look at the exterior of the motel, followed Elena into room one.

It stank of smoke. Boxes, opened and unopened, were piled against all four walls, stacked at varying heights. She'd known that Elena had decided to live in the motel when she bought it, like many owners before her. What she didn't know was how little progress had been made on the unpacking. If it wasn't for the made bed or the books, jewelry, and pills piled on little tables, Marcia would have thought Elena had arrived only hours ago. The longer she stared at the boxes, the more details emerged. Marcia noted the objects and herbs used to ward away evil: talismans and garlic. But what concerned Marcia most was the cross hanging above the bed.

"Elena," Marcia said, throwing her chin toward it. "You do know the approach I take to my work, don't you?"

"Oh, that was my brother. He insisted. I don't believe, but I figured, eh, what's the harm? If the big man wants to help me out, I'm not gonna complain."

"I see."

It wasn't that Marcia didn't want to believe. She would be open to God, if God decided to present Himself. Only,

His holiness had never shown up. It was this rejection of belief that meant Marcia had always struggled to explain what she did. At first it was a combination of buzzwords and explanations until, eventually, she'd coined the term Nextorcist.

A more progressive exorcist.

The goals were the same, to rid a place of evil, but where an exorcist would call on holy water and dusty verse to force evil from its home, Marcia used her talent and science, drawing on the belief that the best way to get evil out was to reason with it and strike a deal.

"Now, Elena, before I begin, I want to ask you something. Have you personally experienced anything odd here? Anything supernatural or unexplainable?"

"No. I've had some weird dreams, but, believe it or not, most of the grief I've had about Waxwing Creek comes from people."

"Customers?" Marcia asked.

"People from Hunt. They can't understand why a woman would up and move to a place like this with hopes of turning it around."

"Why did you?"

"Because I got divorced," Elena said dryly. "I figured a haunted motel couldn't be worse than my ex-husband."

Marcia nodded. "And do you plan on changing the name? I've always wondered why, through all its trauma, it's remained as Waxwing Creek."

"There's a note in the deed," Elena said, "from Cliff and Annabelle, the two that opened it. I mean, what're they gonna do if we change it? Nothing, of course. But I guess I, and others before me, keep the name as a sign of respect... after what happened, you know?"

"I see. Is anyone staying here tonight?"

"Nope. Made sure you had the place to yourself."

"I appreciate that," Marcia said.

Beside her, Elena lit another cigarette. She did it with a match and took in a drag so heavy Marcia heard the tobacco crackle.

"There are owners who would have thrown you out for that."

"For what?"

"Smoking inside. Walt Crane, one of the first, after Cliff and Annabelle. He hated that."

"You've done your research." Elena smiled. "Can I get you anything before you start?"

"A coffee would be lovely. After that, I'll begin."

When Elena brought Marcia her coffee, Marcia was at the edge of the room, moving the curtains apart with a long fingernail so she could peer into the woods outside.

"Thank you," she whispered, using the cup to warm her hands. Already, she felt something here. Energy. Memories. Trauma. She felt a presence, scratching at the surface, begging to come in. She didn't know why it was asking. Not yet. But she would. As soon as she opened herself up to it. As soon as she opened the floodgates, she'd know.

"So, tell me, Elena. What exactly do you want to achieve today? What is an ideal scenario for you?"

"Honestly?" She paused, flicking her cigarette into the ashtray beside her bed. "Clarity. Answers. Some sort of substance to what exactly I've taken on here. I've got so many people telling me their own version of events, so many stories being thrown around, that I'm struggling to figure out what's real."

"And then?"

"And then, if you do find anything, I want you to offer it

an invitation to get out," Elena said. "I want to be the one that breaks Waxwing Creek's curse."

"I understand," Marcia said.

"I do have a good feeling there's *something* here. Not every place comes with so much—"

"History," Marcia finished her sentence, then took a slow sip of her coffee. It tasted more bitter than she liked it. "Do you have sugar?"

"Oh, yes," Elena said, moving across the room to rummage in one of the boxes. "I'm sorry," she commented, shaking a packet to force its crystals to the bottom. "I've been so nervous about you coming. After seeing that interview you did, I almost canceled. Didn't know you were so in demand."

"Well," Marcia said, ripping the packet in one smooth motion before tipping its contents into her cup. "I'm glad you didn't."

And she was glad. The motel had a reputation. It had put the work in. Spent years building a name for itself and had the stories and body count to match. This place thrived on ruthlessness but had, in some dark, twisted way, earned respect for it. Marcia knew the two balanced on a tipping point. This was the place where people had killed and had been killed. This is where people came to live and ended up dying. One wrong move—one more death—could turn it from a business to a museum.

Marcia emptied the last dregs of her cup, savoring the sweetness gathered at the bottom. "Okay," she announced. "I think it's time we found out what's going on at Waxwing Creek."

Marcia asked Elena to leave—take a drive—and had breathed a sigh of relief when she agreed. It wasn't uncommon to see the desperation in their eyes. Elena wanted answers, and it was Marcia's job to make that happen, but she felt better doing it alone.

Since Elena left, Marcia had spent time in every part of the motel, moving from room to room, corner to corner, walking its interior and exterior. She had an EMF meter for reading the fluctuations of electromagnetic fields. A thermal camera for the heat. Typically, she didn't like using them. She preferred to rely on the talent, or intuition, she was born with, and it had only taken one loop of the structure for her to decide that would be the case here. Whatever rested here rested uneasy. The sensation of death was strong. She wouldn't need technology to coax it out.

So she'd decided to use a camera, which had been rolling the whole time, recording the words Marcia had been speaking into it. As she completed her second loop of Waxwing Creek's exterior, she re-entered Elena's room. The smell of stale smoke hit her, and she pushed open the window so she could focus. She rested the camera on a pile of boxes, readjusting it so the lens faced the bed, readying herself for whatever she was about to invite in.

She breathed in, settled her lungs, her nerves, and then opened herself up to it.

It, whatever *it* was, was on her as soon as she summoned it. It felt heavy and wet, like a thick, gelatinous tongue crawling into her mouth. She reminded herself she was a nextorcist. Here to talk—to reason—but instinct told her that wasn't going to happen.

In its mass she saw visions, dark and messy. She tried to decipher them, the movements, colors, and sounds. She saw cars with cut wires, blood on bingo paper. She heard music and saw walls running red. There was a man too. Someone like her. Someone who could communicate with the dead. Those were just the loudest, the most prominent, making themselves known through a gloom of dirty conversations and bodies bound together by money, drugs, and sex.

Caught in its thrum of madness, Marcia understood why Waxwing Creek had a reputation. Elena wanted better for it, and she respected her for that, but the thing she was faced with didn't want better. There were flashes of brilliance and rare moments of hope, but as a mass, this monster, this *thing*, huge and overwhelming, filling up Waxwing Creek with its sludge, wanted things to remain *exactly* as they were.

Still, she held firm, knowing there would be a source. No matter the state, there was always an anchor tying the chaos in place. So, she pushed. Pushed through the sludge to find out where it was coming from—or what was rooting it down.

She forced herself forward, squeezing her body through what felt like cold creases of flesh, acutely aware that it wanted her to leave. She pressed until she'd breached its other side and realized she wasn't in the motel at all. She was outside.

She looked behind her, and Waxwing Creek stood, illuminated, as a warm and golden glow. It looked holy, glorious, like an oasis of light in all that dark. She asked it to show her the anchor. She willed the place to open itself to her.

Show me so we can talk.

The motel rearranged itself. She watched its walls collapse and rebuild themselves into a house. Its dark front drooped, gaping like a mouth. As soon as she saw it, Marcia knew what it was, and she knew who lived there.

"Dakota."

She whispered it to herself, wondering whether the voice would make it to the real world, where she was seated on a bed, eyes rolled to white, surrounded by boxes and stale cigarette smoke.

She made her way to the house, using her legs to separate the material that leaked out of the property's orifices. The closer she got, the more the material changed, turning from a sticky substance to cold, wet leaves.

The rest of the forest, dark and wet, hummed around her. The property sat in the middle of it, a piece of land cut out of its ink. The trunks of the trees looked like stiff limbs, with long-fingered branches and leaves that glistened with their own putrid glow. She squinted, trying to make out what those glows were, aware that some were flittering, twitching.

She continued to skirt the house's exterior. Out of its windows and around its doors poured the dark leaves. All except one window that sat alone, unguarded, on the ground floor at the back of the house.

Marcia moved closer, seeing shadows casting themselves out of it, and hearing the sound of hurried voices within.

When she reached it, she peered through and saw a family seated around a wooden table, worry plastered onto their weathered faces.

"And you're telling me the truth? You swear to God you saw what you saw?"

"I promise!" The young girl—the man's daughter—was distressed. "I thought they were the leaves. The reflection of our lights. But they were eyes. I'm telling you, they moved."

"Did they talk to you? Did these eyes tell you anything?"

"Yes."

"What did they tell you?"

"They...they told me I should try something. Do something. Something bad. But I didn't! I didn't listen."

"Alright," the man grumbled. "You all wait here."

"George," the woman cried. "Please."

"Sit down, Mary. Watch the kids. And bolt that door behind me."

Marcia watched as he moved to the rifle in the corner. She wondered if they could see the leaves crawling up the walls, breaking through creaking floorboards, or how those leaves swallowed the light.

George picked up the rifle, splitting the back apart to slide a bullet into the chamber.

"George," the woman cried, trying again. "Just stay in the house, for God's sake. Wait until morning at least."

"I'm not waiting till morning. This is *my* house. *My* land. And I defy whatever it is out there to tell me otherwise."

When he slammed the door behind him, Marcia moved away from the window, watching as the wall of inky leaves split for him as he left, rifle in hands, for the forest.

"For too long you've plagued this family," Marcia heard him shout. She followed the voice, straining to trace its echo. She looked behind her, cursing as Dakota House faded out of sight, swallowed by the thickness of crooked branches and leaves.

"For too long you've haunted this place. You can do whatever you want to me. But when you start on my children and my wife, the games stop."

Marcia followed, pulling her trousers over her ankles and her sleeves down her arms, aware of the branches licking at her skin. The faster she moved, the thicker the forest grew. Before, the leaves had been small and copious. Now, they were large, their surfaces rough and worn like leather, and she saw the girl had been right. It wasn't a reflection of light on those leaves. They were eyes. Thousands of them, surrounded by tiny rows of teeth, and each was open, watching her every move. With a single, wet sweep, they shifted, readjusting their gaze as she moved deeper into the forest.

She tried to ignore them. Tried so hard to not catch any of their stares.

Eventually, she found George standing behind trunks that looked like bars of a prison cell. She watched him lift the rifle, push its butt into the cushion of his shoulder, and fire off a round. The bullet split the leaves, splintering one of the branches, blowing hundreds of little eyes apart.

Marcia heard him reload, but before he had the chance to fire again, she saw him lower the weapon and stare. She couldn't see what he was looking at. Couldn't see what he was lost in. All she saw was his eyes wide and his mouth open, desperate for escape, and then he turned and ran.

Marcia gave chase, feeling the leaves biting at her as the ground slipped from under her feet. The forest erupted in a flurry of alien cries and the sound of breaking wood. She wondered how she was ever going to find her way back, but then the house appeared, as ominous as it was before. The window that had glowed before was now dark, its hole now weeping fresh leaves. She smelled stale smoke, felt the room at Waxwing Creek breaking in around her, and knew her time here was almost up. She hadn't even begun to reason with what nestled here, and already, the real world was calling her back.

George was nowhere to be seen. Unsure what to do, she circled the structure, trying to find a new way inside. She thought back to her research, filtering through everything she knew about Waxwing Creek and Dakota House: all its notes, photographs, and stories.

And then it dawned on her. The attic. Stories of a family lined up and shot, alone but together.

She put everything into climbing to the top of Dakota House. Spent every ounce of strength on finding footholds in roots and pulling herself up with fingers that slipped off leaves with eyes and teeth.

When she reached it, the attic's window was small and covered with filth. She pressed her fingers into the slippery mass, snapping her nails, splitting the skin, willing the darkness to part. She knew whatever was here was desperate to stop her, but she persisted until the leafy curtain parted, and she could look through the slit she'd created.

"Please, George," his wife moaned, on her knees. "Don't do this. The kids."

"There's nothing good in this world," he whispered. "Nothing good."

Around Marcia's fingers, the sludge grew barbs that cut her and bloomed poisonous colors that would make her insides bleed.

She saw George ready the rifle. Saw him load the first bullet.

But then he turned and looked at her, and she saw desperate sadness—or was it madness?—in his eyes. He fixed his gaze on her, moved toward her, and she tried to push away. Tried to escape leaves that stuck to her fingers like glue.

The barrel of the weapon reached out of the slit and pointed its darkness at Marcia's forehead. Before she could scream, before she could beg him to stop, George pulled the trigger and released the bullet into her brain.

Marcia regained consciousness. Her head was thumping. She moved her neck, wincing as pain shot down her back and across her temples.

"Marcia?" The voice was thick and fuzzy. "Marcia? Marcia, are you alright?"

Marcia remembered she was working. At the church? The newspaper? She was a journalist. A good one. No, a motel. *The* motel. Waxwing Creek. And then she remembered the voice belonged to Elena Charr, and she recalled darkness oozing out of a house like pus and how hard it had been to get there.

Marcia groaned, struggling as she pushed herself up on her elbows.

"Here, let me help you."

Marcia wanted to say no but was worried opening her mouth would make her pass out. She kept her eyes closed, focused on pushing away the queasiness, doing nothing as she felt the woman's hands find their way under her armpits. The support helped more than she wanted to admit, and she leaned on Elena's strength to move her onto one of the room's chairs.

She put her head in her hands, using fingers to massage the temples. The sound of Elena asking if she was alright again didn't help. Neither did the fact she was lighting a cigarette.

"Can I get you anything?"

"Water," was all Marcia could manage. Her mouth was dry.

"Here," Elena said, wrapping Marcia's hand around the cup.

Marcia took it to her lips, expecting to take a sip but

downing it. It eased the throbbing, and Elena disappeared to get another.

"What happened?" Elena asked as she returned. "I came back and you were just lying there passed out. I thought you'd fallen asleep. I thought..."

"The camera," Marcia struggled, holding out a shaking finger.

Elena moved, grabbed the camera, and gave it to her.

With strained breaths and limited movements, Marcia used her fingers to click around the interface and rewind the last minutes.

The footage showed what Marcia suspected: Herself, in a state of unconsciousness, gripped by what was happening in another realm. That video would offer no clues. Whatever had happened there would have to come back to Marcia in fragments, across time, in moments she would least expect. For now, all she had was footage of her looking gray, shaking, and then collapsing. Nothing more. Nothing less.

Marcia sighed, letting the camera drop into her lap, tilting her head back so she could breathe better. "They should have never built that house."

"Who?"

"The Dakotas. They should have never cut out a space in this forest to build a home for themselves."

"Marcia, what are you talking about?"

"The trees. It's in the trees."

"I don't understand."

"The thing that has haunted this place for all these years." She sighed, her voice tired and defeated. "It's in the trees. It *is* the trees."

Marcia took a moment to steady herself. She closed her eyes, taking another sip of her drink.

"But what does that have to do with Waxwing Creek?"

"It has *everything* to do with Waxwing Creek."

Marcia watched the woman. Saw the hope leave her eyes. Saw the last motes of happiness blown from her face.

"But you can get it out, right? You can ask it to leave?"

Marcia shook her head.

"But that's why I asked you to come here. That's what you do!"

"Elena, you can't ask an entire forest to leave."

"Well, reason with it then. Strike a deal."

"Some things you just can't reason with."

"I don't believe this."

"When Cliff and Annabelle opened this place, they disturbed something, like the Dakotas did before them. Something that calls to people. Something that plays with people. Tests them. Encourages their worst. Only, the Dakotas kept it to their house, to their family and their property. Whether by accident or not, Cliff and Annabelle invited others into its mess."

"So, what exactly are you trying to tell me?"

"I'm telling you to go, Elena. I'm telling you to run. Because as long as Waxwing Creek is standing, people will come. The more you or anyone else tries to change it—the more you try and fix it—the more danger you're going to put yourself in. Whatever is out there likes this motel. It's happy with its lot, and it'll do all it can to ensure nothing about that changes. So if you value your life, if you don't want to find yourself caught up in other people's messes, you'll put this fresh start behind you. You'll leave. You'll leave and never, ever look back."

THE KNOCKS WERE soft but delivered with purpose. Marcia put down her book, her coffee, and opened the door to two smart-looking but solemn police officers, young enough to be her children.

"Ms. Martins?"

"Yes?"

"My name's Joe. This here is Remy. We're from Hunt Police Department. Can we come in?"

"Hunt?" Marcia exclaimed, confusion clear on her face. "What are you doing out here?"

"We'd like to come in," Joe continued, looking over Marcia's shoulder to the house's interior. "If we can?"

"We just want to ask a few questions," Remy said.

"Alright." Marcia nodded. "Sure."

She led them to the living room, moving the book she had open on the sofa so they could sit. "Can I get you anything? Tea? Coffee?"

"No, no, that won't be necessary," Joe said, perching on the edge of the sofa next to Remy. Marcia leaned against a cabinet on the other end of the room, crossing her arms.

"So," she said, "what is it? What's happened?"

"Do you know a woman called Elena Charr?"

"Yes... Well, sort of. I wouldn't say I *know* her. She needed help with something at the motel she owns. Waxwing Creek. I visited about a month ago, though, being from Hunt, I'm guessing you already know that."

"Elena was found dead this morning," Remy said. With a voice as soft as that, Marcia wondered whether she was always the one who announced bad news.

"What?" Marcia's brow creased. "Where?"

"In her room at Waxwing Creek."

"Oh my God," Marcia gasped, hand resting around her throat. She thought back to her visit. The things she'd seen.

The hurt she'd felt. The visions she'd experienced. She'd told the woman to turn away. She'd encouraged the woman to leave. Why hadn't she listened?

"What happened?"

"We're still figuring out the specifics," Joe said. "All we know is that she changed the name of the place from Waxwing Creek to Rester's Lodge a few days ago. Had a whole renovation planned. We're hoping you'll be able to answer a few questions."

"Of course. Anything you need."

"Alright—"

"But before I do, I need to know something," Marcia said. "How did she die?"

Joe hesitated.

"Ms. Martins," he began, "we can't share those details."

"You can," she said. "Of course you can. Tell me how she died."

The officers shared a look, and Marcia knew they were deliberating on whether to tell her. Deliberating until, finally, they did.

"To tell you the truth," Joe said, cautiously, "we don't know. She was in such a...unique state when we found her, we're struggling to figure out the events that led to her passing."

"What do you mean?"

"It was the state of her body," Remy said, shaking her head. "The bones. Ms. Martins, her spine had been pulled out of her mouth."

ACKNOWLEDGMENTS

My biggest thanks go to those who stayed at Waxwing Creek first.

To Emily Grandy and Brandi Stokes, whose notes and feedback were instrumental in making these stories better. To Renee DeCamillis, whose approach to editing didn't just improve this collection, but made me a better writer.

To my partner, Joanna, family, and friends, for their unwavering support and encouragement to write.

And, as always, to you, for reading.

ABOUT THE AUTHOR

J.J. Walker is a horror author who loves writing unsettling stories about small towns, old houses, and characters that examine what it means to be human. Originally from the UK, he currently calls Canada home.

His debut novel, *BURIED BY SUNSET*, was published in 2023.

www.ingramcontent.com/pod-product-compliance
Lightning Source LLC
Chambersburg PA
CBHW021718190726
48289CB00008B/2582